Flowers of the Dinh Ba Forest

a novel by

Robert David Clark

Livingston Press
at
The University of West Alabama

ISBN 1-931982-29-5 library binding
ISBN 1-931982-30-9, trade paper
Library of Congress Control Number 2003114282

Printed on acid-free paper.
Printed in the United States of America by:
Publishers' Graphics, LLC
Hardcover binding by: Heckman Bindery

Typesetting and page layout: Heather Leigh Loper
Proofreading: Tomekia Walker, Daphne Moore,
      Charles Loveless, Jessica Meigs, Gina Montarsi
Cover design: Josh Dewberry, Gina Montarsi
Cover photos:
      Tower Photo by kind permission of John Foster
      Orchid Photo by kind permission of W. H. Bandisch
      Soldier Photo by Unknown from www.nixonlibrary.com

The poem "Elegy," by Bruce Weigl,
is from *Song of Napalm* and is used with kind permission of the author.

I want to thank the following people, without whom this book would not be possible: Stephen Slimp and Joe Taylor at the University of West Alabama. Terry Davis, who long ago told me I could. Damion Higbie and Matt Mauch for those great summer nights above the Square Deal. Eddie Micus for never letting me forget it always comes down to language. Mike Lohre for being the kind of guy I'm always happy to see. And for hand-rolled cigars, handguns, and Harley-Davidsons, my friend Jim Petersen. Oh, yeah, and for "Case The Wonder Dog," the best damned hound a man could ask for.

This is a work of fiction.
You know the rest: any resemblance
to persons living or dead is coincidental.

Livingston Press is part of The University of West Alabama,
and thereby has non-profit status.
Donations are tax-deductible:
brothers and sisters, we need 'em.
first edition
6 5 4 3 3 2 1

For Courtney and Heather

This book is dedicated to the memory of

Robert M. Flanigan.

Killed in action, April 29, 1969.

1968
The year of the monkey

At first light, outside the village of Xon Dao, Sau Ban waited alone on a paddy dike, wishing for rain. He liked the cool, slick feel of rain on his skin. Its smell in the first hours of morning always reminded him of home. When he was young, Sau Ban would watch rain flatten the dust in the city's streets. He liked how the water gathered to form brown rivers beside the curbs. He'd build boats out of tamarind leaves and drop them in the rushing water, watching until they were out of sight, imagining the places they went, the sights he might see if he were small enough to ride along. The French had been in Hue when he was young, the French and their love of parades. It seemed they never grew tired of marching through the old imperial city.

Overhead, the gray sky was still. The rice fields played out in mis-matched shapes of emerald green, the treelines surrounding them were locked in shadow. Dew-laden rice plants held the morning light in a blanket of silver. Off to the west a bank of charcoal-colored clouds rose steadily upward from the horizon. Rain. Not yet, but in a while.

A few days ago the sky had opened up and emptied itself for hours on the village. The morning had been perfect.

A young soldier had stumbled into Sau Ban's camp. He wore a uniform of the Army of the Republic of Vietnam. Sau Ban knew he was a deserter, and to his way of thinking this made the ARVN the lowest form of life imaginable. Sau Ban could not tolerate cowardice or dereliction of duty from a soldier. It was a matter of honor, and Sau Ban believed himself an honorable man. And desertion? If the deserter also happened to be the enemy, then the crime became so vile that Sau Ban honestly felt cheated by not being able to kill him twice.

Since he'd been in the delta, the opportunity to take a prisoner had never before presented itself, and after Sau Ban beat the boy senseless with a rifle butt, he ordered his men to drag him farther into the treeline. He didn't want to kill the boy right away. He needed time to think. It seemed a shame to waste the spectacle of an execution on a audience of four. While he considered the situation, Sau Ban amused himself by pretending to load his automatic pistol. When he pressed the barrel against the boy's forehead and pulled the trigger on the empty chamber, the boy's bowels flushed. Sau Ban spit on the prisoner, sniffing the air with contempt and berating him for being a coward. He ordered the boy stripped and bound by his hands and feet to a bamboo pole. At Sau Ban's direction a length of filthy cloth was ripped from the back of the boy's pants and used to gag him.

A short time later, the problem of where to shoot the boy solved itself. Tuan, Sau Ban's latest recruit, admitted to knowing the prisoner after the boy had called out Tuan's name. It turned out they were from the same village. But a few moments later, Tuan regretted his honesty.

Without further delay, Sau Ban made plans to haul the boy back to Xon Dao. What would be better, he asked his men, than to execute the boy in his own village. It was nearly too good to be true.

Tuan and another man lifted the pole to their shoulders, and the group set off, the prisoner swaying between them like a pig on his way to market. With each bounce of the pole, Tuan felt sick to his stomach. He wanted to drop the boy and run. But he was too frightened of Sau Ban to do anything but follow the man in front of him.

The five men and their prisoner traveled for most of the night by keeping close to the treelines, only moving out into the open paddies when necessary. A little before daylight they arrived at the village, and set up in a small stand of trees to wait for dawn. Whenever the prisoner stirred or made a sound, Sau Ban kicked him in the head until he was quiet.

Tuan pretended to sleep, hoping Sau Ban might doze long enough for him to sneak away, but Sau Ban never allowed himself to get comfortable. He spent the time between beatings by watching the sky, and listening for sounds of the enemy. There were none.

Morning brought a heavy rain that rattled the palm frond treetops and caused the rice plants to bend in the paddies. The soft ground at Sau Ban's feet quickly soaked up the moisture, replacing it with the stench of moldering decay.

When the clouded sky grew light enough to see, Sau Ban led Tuan and the rest from their hiding place and onto the large dike that ran through the center of Xon Dao.

With a sense of foreboding Tuan stared at the twenty brown palm huts of his home village. They were set ten to a side, each looking like supports on a low-slung bridge. Chickens pecked for grit in the center of the village, and white ducks swam among the paddy rice. In a circular holding pen, a water buffalo snorted and pawed the ground at the smell of the men.

The prisoner's eyes were swollen shut from Sau Ban's continuous beatings, and sometime during the night the leeches had found him. At least twelve leeches, puffed up to three times their original size, dangled here and there from the boy's chest and legs. One had slithered into his nostril so that only the tail could be seen. Several of them fell to the mud when Tuan and his partner jostled the pole to a more comfortable position on their shoulders.

Tuan looked to see Sau Ban's reaction, but there was none, only an emotionless expression so void of life that Tuan looked away. He knew Sau Ban's desire to make a name for himself during his stay in the Mekong River Delta. And Tuan knew Sau Ban was determined to build a reputation so great it would be passed from village to village, province to province, until word of his exploits was noticed by the fools in the North who had sent him to run with this rag-tag band of children. Those were Sau Ban's exact words, for by now Tuan knew them well. Several times Tuan had been forced to listen while Sau Ban screamed tirades about the injustice of it all, seeming to grow angrier each time the subject came up.

Sau Ban would sometimes reminisce how after he came south, he spent the first few weeks in Saigon, making and planting bombs. But the life of a terrorist—hiding by day, blowing up theaters and bars at night—hadn't suited him. Sau Ban told the men he believed this work unfitting for a man of his caliber. He considered himself a warrior, and wanted to meet the enemy head on in battle, not by killing them with anonymous explosions.

Because of this, Sau Ban said, he left Saigon and headed into the delta alone. But he knew he wouldn't be alone for long. Before their departure from the North, Sau Ban and the men traveling with him were given the names of contacts in the South, members of the Viet Cong who would provide them with identification, money, food, and weapons.

Sau Ban liked to boast that he only hit the Americans when it suited him, when it was to his advantage. The engagment might last no more than a few minutes before he would break contact with the enemy, and vanish into the jungle ahead of their forth-coming air-strikes and artillery, leaving them to blow holes in the thick vegetation, a snake or two, but little else. Sau Ban and his men were always outnumbered, and it took courage to engage the American soldiers in close combat. But his men would fight none-theless, because each knew what Tuan knew. Their chances of sur-viving the war were over if Sau Ban suspected them of cowardice in the face of the enemy. He had promised to kill any man who ran or hesitated, and like the rest, Tuan had no reason to doubt Sau Ban's resolve.

One day, in a fleeting moment of reflection, even Sau Ban ad-mitted that some might call his actions atrocities. But he had waved the notion away just as quickly. Let others call it what they liked, he said, showing one of his rare smiles, he called it war.

The villagers were roused from their homes and told to gather in the center of the village. A few minutes later, forty-two people squatted in the pouring rain while Sau Ban paced before them, the prisoner hanging on display to his rear.

Tuan's eyes wavered between Sau Ban and his mother, squat-ting among the other villagers, but she wouldn't look at him. And he was glad. He felt ashamed for her to see him like this.

Sau Ban wore nothing more than a pair of black cotton shorts that tied at the waist—his usual attire. The muscles of his chest and arms flexed tightly with each movement. He had a wide, nearly square physique that seemed out of place on a Vietnamese, and he took pride in his strength. He could do pull-ups from a tree branch until his men grew tired of counting. His nose was broad and looked shoved onto his face as an afterthought. His large ears poked mon-key-like from his head, and his dark eyes were always shifting to take in each new situation.

The prisoner's mother was also among the villagers, and when Sau Ban stepped to her son and grabbed a fistful of hair, she at-tempted to rush forward. Only her husband's arms wrapped around her shoulders kept her in place. But Sau Ban wouldn't have harmed her even if she had broken free. He hadn't come to that yet.

With a deft movement, Sau Ban spun on his heels, waved his pistol, and the circle of villagers drew back in one motion. He chambered a round, and the smooth shuttle of steel moving over itself sounded out of place, and at once menacing in the rain-filtered stillness. Only when he was sure that every eye had been turned to him did Sau Ban speak.

"People of Xon Dao," he said in a firm voice. "You will learn that you are either for or against us in our fight against the imperialists!"

He stopped for a minute and pointed to where Tuan stood holding one end of the pole, staring at the ground, unable to look at the faces of people he had known all his life.

"Here you have sent one to aid our struggle. And here," Sau Ban sneered before wheeling around to deliver a kick into the boy's side with a meaty smack from his bare foot. "You have sent one to hinder it."

He waited a moment for his words to die, then continued—and for the villager's benefit, his voice had a new, pleading edge to it, like what he was about to do was something he found distasteful, but necessary.

"Our war for liberation is a hard one. Our sacrifices are great. Do not side with the Americans and their lackeys by sending your children to delay our victory. Do not resist our glorious fight."

With that, he pressed the pistol against the prisoner's temple. When the boy, who until this time had been hanging as limp as if he were already dead, felt the barrel on his battered face he squirmed so violently the pole bounced and shook on Tuan's shoulders.

Sau Ban waited with his fingers wrapped tightly in the boy's hair until his wigglings had ceased. Then, once more Sau Ban pressed the pistol to the side of the boy's head.

"Do not work against the liberation of our homeland by giving aid to the American imperialists! Do not choose to live as traitors, only to die in disgrace!"

The shot that followed was a muffled pop, and the sound of it surprised even Sau Ban. It was as if the pistol had blown its noise into the boy's brain. Sau Ban wondered if it were loud to the boy, or had he even heard? He was honestly curious and wished he could ask. Blood geysered from the hole in the boy's head, then his body gave a final shudder.

With a nod from Sau Ban, Tuan and the man holding the other end slipped the pole from their shoulders and the body dropped with a heavy splat. The villagers stared at their feet, at the mud and water gathering around them. No one moved until Sau Ban spoke, and then each villager reluctantly raised their eyes to him.

"When the lackeys come looking for their lost pup, you tell them it was Sau Ban who did this. And that he will do the same to each of them."

Sau Ban and his men remained in the village for another hour, eating and stocking up on what food there was. In each household, Sau Ban announced he would be returning in a few days to collect a tax. When any of the villagers found the courage to complain, Sau Ban scolded them like an angry father for their selfishness, or frightened them with accusations about their loyalties.

Meanwhile, in his home, Tuan was allowed to visit with his mother whom he hadn't seen since Sau Ban came for him a little over two months ago. His mother fixed him a meal of rice and *noucmam*, a sauce made from the drippings of drying fish. Tuan ate several bowls of it without speaking.

After finishing his third bowl down to the last grain, he wiped his mouth with the back of his hand, then hurried to his khaki pack and rifle lying in the doorway. He returned to the table carrying a small wooden box, a long blade of grass tied neatly around it to hold the lid in place. Tuan set the gift on the table and took his seat again.

"For you," he said, nudging the box toward her.

Despite the situation, his mother smiled like a school girl. "What is this, Tuan?"

"Why not look?" he said, enjoying the expression on her face.

Inside the box were three dark brown beans, each nearly three inches long and as thick as her little finger. A sweet, fruity smell rose from the box, filling the air above the table.

His mother held one of the rubbery beans between the fingers of both hands and gave him a quizzical look.

"I have been to a place where flowers grow up the sides of trees until they reach the top. These beans grow on them."

"What kind of place is this?"

Tuan knew his mother liked to hear about new places. She had never been more than a few miles from the village her entire life.

"Sau Ban says it is the Dinh Ba Forest."

She pointed east. "That way?"

"No," Tuan said, shaking his head and motioning in the opposite direction. "The Plain of Reeds. The forest is there. But we have traveled in all directions. Sau Ban keeps us moving. The American soldiers are everywhere. Once we walked for five days and only stopped because we had reached the sea."

At the mention of this her face grew thoughtful, and she cupped a hand over the tight roll of black hair at the back of her head, squeezing it the way Tuan knew she did when considering matters. He also knew his grandfather had told her stories of men who fished the sea, the boats they used, the way the water was as blue as the sky. His mother once told Tuan she couldn't imagine water that color, nor could she picture waves higher than a house, or sand the color of rice.

"Tuan, you have seen it?"

He nodded. "Through the trees. I wanted to put my feet in it, but Sau Ban forbid me to."

"What color is it?"

"Blue."

"Like the sky?"

"Yes," he said, softly. "Like the sky, only bluer."

In a few more minutes it was time to go. Tuan didn't know where Sau Ban was taking them next, but promised to return as soon as he could. After planting a wet kiss on his mother's forehead, he grabbed his rifle and pack, then bolted from the house to join the men waiting for him at the edge of the trees.

Part One

Chapter 1

Leon heard the patter of rain approaching through the paddies, but still had barely enough time to pull the poncho over himself before the first drops landed. Rain here was like nothing he'd seen before. It rarely sprinkled, or fell in a mist. Every cloud seemed incapable of holding its water if he happened to be below it. Out here in the paddies, Leon thought of it as like being on a weird lake. A shallow, mud-water brown, checkered lake, or at least that was how it appeared to him the first time he'd seen the terrain from the air. And in some ways it wasn't so much different than home without the water. Instead of elm, oak, and cottonwood trees meandering through the fields of Iowa farm country, here there were acres of coconut palm, banana, and betel trees to break up the rice paddies. Dense stands of nipa palm rose everywhere from the banks of the canals and streams coursing the delta, creating undergrowth difficult to walk through, and taller than a man's head. But it was the climate that caught everyone's attention. The first time Leon set foot in-country, he'd stood in the doorway of the air-conditioned airplane gasping for breath in the heat-fired humidity of the place. And for days after, he felt as though he were being gradually smothered under a warm moist towel. It was impossible to drink enough water, and he hadn't known a moment without thirst.

Off in the middle distance, the tiny village of Xon Dao all but disappeared from sight when the rain passed over it. Leon watched with a twinge of longing, envying the people there sleeping warm and dry. He thought of home, of chilly dark mornings lying in bed, the window open, while rain splashed over the clogged gutters of his parent's house. He remembered pulling the covers under his chin and falling back to a safe sleep, which was what he missed more than anything. Sleep. After ten months in-country he felt like he'd been awake the entire time.

With his head tipped against the rain Leon fired the day's first Marlboro to life with a Zippo, which had the outline of Vietnam etched into one side, *Fuck The Army* inscribed on the other. He cupped the end of the cigarette and took a long pull, letting smoke slip from his lips and up his nose. Leon's green eyes narrowed to slits at the smell, like a dog catching the first scent of something potent on a passing breeze.

Behind him, strung out in lumpy gray piles on the two-foot-wide dike, the rest of the squad lay in what passed for sleep. Their heads were on rucksacks and covered with olive-drab towels to ward off the swarming mosquitoes. When the first drops of rain fell, each of the men stirred and drew the ponchos over their grubby faces.

Last evening the six of them arrived on foot, and after moving into a treeline, they made a false lager, waiting for nightfall. Once darkness fell they moved four-hundred meters into the paddies where they arranged an L-shaped ambush beside a wide dike known as a candy-stripe for its red-and-white designation on their maps. The dike was thick enough to carry carts of rice during the day: weapons and men at night. During the night the men had taken two hour watches, each calling in negative sit-reps on the hour. They observed nothing, and with the exception of some small-arms fire in the distance, and a gunship blasting at something near the horizon, the night passed quietly.

The rain ended quickly, leaving behind a humid fog hovering over the paddies that would soon burn away. Out of habit, Leon kept an eye on the treelines while he smoked. Without the sun shining on them, the trees surrounding him weren't glowing that particularly brilliant shade of green, a color so intense it actually appeared to vibrate.

From the corner of his eye he caught movement. Beside the village a man stopped with one hand against a hut before hiking up a leg of his faded black shorts and relieving himself into a paddy. At the same time, with a turtle-like move, Preacher poked his grimy face from beneath his poncho.

"What's the time?" Preacher said, his nose snorting in short bursts at a mosquito that wanted to land on it.

"O-six-hundred," Leon answered, not taking his eyes from the man who seemed to be pissing enough for three people.

Preacher sat up and looked around as if he were seeing the area for the first time. He'd gotten four hours sleep, but looked none the better for it. There was a slouch to his shoulders, and he looked like a man who had already put in a day's work.

Leon glanced from the village and down at a mosquito, blood red and smack in the middle of Preacher's wide forehead. His chin was square, his nose thick and straight. He had blue eyes, and reddish-blonde hair. Preacher looked like a Viking, which is what he claimed to be the descendent of.

Leon peeked back to the pissing man, but he was gone.

Getting to his knees, Preacher wiped a hand over his face. Mosquito blood and the grime of last night's repellent smeared down his cheeks. He unfastened his fatigues and let them drop to the dike. A moment later and an arc of piss landed five feet out in the paddy with the sound of water poured from a can. Preacher was short, with sturdy shoulders and barrel legs, the stoutest man in the platoon. Seeing Preacher with his pants down, Leon couldn't help but stare at the half-dollar-sized red welts that covered his legs from knee to crotch. Some were bleeding.

"Doc know about the ringworm, Preach?"

Preacher shook his head, face turned to the sky, eyes closed in relief. He spoke stiffly, as if pissing required his full concentration.

"I'm waiting for it to get bad enough."

He itched the fingers of both hands along his thighs for long blissful seconds, then gingerly lifted his scrotum and scratched there for a good while. After zipping up, Preacher plopped down on the dike, his feet submerged in paddy water, staring down at them in a thoughtful pose.

Leon kept silent, not that he had anything much he wanted to talk about.

Back in the world, Elston Lohre was the son of a Lutheran minister in Willow, Minnesota, but everyone here called him Preacher. He'd been a college boy at South Dakota State in the winter of '67. There he met a girl who worked the four-to-midnight shift as a security guard at the college. One thing led to another, and late one night while giving her the business on a desk top in one of the English Department offices, a teaching assistant, who'd been asleep on a couch in another office, stepped in and caught Preacher in mid-stroke. It wasn't the first time they'd fucked in the office, but it would be their last. A few weeks later— after the chairwoman of the department sent a registered letter informing Preacher's draft board of his dismissal from higher education—his Selective Service status changed to 1A.

"I had to get away from my old man," Preacher once told Leon while speaking on everyone's favorite subject, home. "He sort of went goofy after that."

Still, Preacher hadn't lost his faith. The words *Christian Soldier* arched over the drawing of a smiley-face on the front of his helmet. He prayed often and openly. He was likable and easy to get along with. Preacher had a way of making a person comfortable in his company. It was his intelligence, an intellect born of common sense. In a place where common sense seemed to be an afterthought, a guy like Preacher was nice to have around.

By now, plumes of white cooking-fire smoke were curling above the rooftops and trees of the village. Leon watched the smoke fade into the low clouds and felt a familiar misery enter him. He'd always been amazed at how beautiful this country could seem one moment, only to explode into grotesque shapes the next. The kind of place where two days before, a boy riding atop a grazing water buffalo—who smiled and posed calendar-like as the men passed in the afternoon—was ambushed by them later that night while he headed out to string booby-traps. The next morning Leon found the boy, half-submerged in paddy water, a ragged hole in the middle of his chest. Lying next to him was a kit bag of fishing line, some empty C-ration cans, and two grenades.

"What's for breakfast, Mother?" Preacher said just then, reaching into his ruck for a moment and coming up with a can of C-rations.

Leon gave him another passing glance, then faced the village once more.

"Know what bothers me more than anything about this place, Leon?"

Leon shrugged, while Preacher opened a can of chopped ham and eggs. Preacher had to be the only person Leon knew who could eat the stuff. Even the kids who begged the soldiers for food refused to take it.

"There aren't any birds," Preacher said. "I think that bothers me more than anything."

Preacher rolled a marble-sized chunk of C4 between his palms while he talked. He placed it on the dike, set a match to it, and the plastic explosive turned into a ball of blue flame. Preacher rotated the can over the tiny fire and said: "All this vegetation and there ain't one bird anywhere."

Leon's eyes searched the treelines like he might be able to see one. But he knew Preacher was right. There weren't any birds, a fact the two of them had discussed on more than one occasion, and it never failed to leave Leon a little homesick.

"I miss that," Preacher said. "I like to hear birds in the morning. Back home the meadowlarks would sing so loud they'd wake me up." He turned the contents of the can over with a white plastic spoon. Steam rose to the surface and Leon soon caught a whiff. He lit another smoke and peered at the village.

"You got meadowlarks back home, Leon?"

Leon nodded.

"Where do you suppose they all went?" Preacher asked, poking a finger in his food to measure the temperature. "Every place has birds, don't it?"

"Maybe the war scared them off."

"I hear they even had elephants," Preacher said around a mouthful of food. "Maybe not down here, but up north. I met this guy from the First Cav on R&R. He told me they saw elephant tracks once. Couldn't see where they came from or where they went. Like it had just been standing there. Weird, huh?"

"Yeah," Leon said, trying to picture the men clustered around the elephant tracks, and happy that Preacher, for the moment at least, had touched on a subject other than birds.

In short order Leon joined Preacher on the dike and opened a can of chicken loaf while trying his best not to let the smell reach his nose. These days he preferred his C's cold. Heat brought out too much of their unique flavor.

"Only birds we got are in these cans I guess, huh, Preach?" Leon said, hoping to make an end of the conversation.

Preacher licked his spoon for a long thoughtful moment, and nodded once as if the fact were well known. "There it is," he said softly, then fixed his eyes on the paddies, focusing on something only he could see.

Leon held his breath and took a wad of chicken, swallowing

after only a few bites, doing his best to ignore the taste. He'd never been so sick of a place, and the lousy food was only part of it. Since coming in-country Leon had tried to believe what they were doing was right, that a reason could be found worth dying for. And at first he'd been able to manage it. But those feelings passed with his innocence. People died suddenly here. No time for last words or good-byes. Alive one moment and dead the next, quickly, often without warning, and that was that. It scared him, that suddenness. His friend Pearl had been given enough time to say something though. Pearl had taken a while to die. He'd looked up at Leon on the trail that day after a booby-trapped mortar round exploded and blew his legs out from under him. Pearl looked up and grabbed for Leon's arm. Not in a desperate way, but like he had something important to tell him. "I've changed my mind." It was the last thing Pearl said, and Leon had been trying to figure out what he'd meant by it ever since.

Something unnamed, but real, was being drained from him with each passing day, from them all, and Leon was without the power to stop any of it. He was frightened: had been for a long time. He couldn't seem to orient himself with the misery of the place, couldn't stay ahead of the sadness. One thing did give him satisfaction. Like a number of men in the platoon he hadn't killed anyone, at least not directly. The platoon's mission seemed to consist of days wandering about waiting for someone to shoot at them. The men rarely saw the enemy unless the enemy wanted them to. When they did make contact, the fire-fight that followed was usually a few sustained minutes of chaotic light, red and green tracers zipping for targets no one could see. Sometimes out of frustration, the men simply shot into the bushes and trees to see if the bushes and trees shot back. But Leon was a good soldier. He followed orders, pulled his weight, and like everyone else, counted the days he had left until that freedom bird came to take him back to the world.

But home to what? He reckoned Herb would most likely give him his old job back if he wanted, but could that be all there was? Spend a year in this godawful place only to go back and pump gas like none of it happened? There was the G.I. Bill, but Leon had never been much for studying anything. He'd graduated damn near at the bottom of his class in high school. What college was going to let him in even if he wanted to go?

Once in Sunday School he'd played the part of Joseph in the Christmas skit. Leon had been nervous for a week, and his mother told him to just keep telling himself to think past it, to think what he would be doing later that day when the skit was over. Leon had imagined lying on the couch after church, basking in his achievement, while he and his father watched football. As it turned out, he wound up lying in his room staring at the ceiling and feeling miserable. He'd bungled his lines so terribly people in the congregation laughed, and no one ever laughed in his church. Leon had done such a good job of blocking out the skit that by the time it came around he was already past it.

Leon knew this place was something impossible to think past, even dangerous to try. Here, a man needed to be aware of what he was doing at the present. The future was never further than the day ahead, and nothing worth looking forward to. On the back of his helmet, written in neat black letters, Leon had summed up his sentiments: *Do to a lack of interest, tomorrow has been cancelled.*

By now the rest of the squad was awake and sitting on the dike. On the other side of Preacher, Conroy and Monroe sat facing opposite directions heating their breakfast over a mutual ball of C4. Sergeant Drieser was a short distance away brushing his teeth. Before rinsing his mouth, he spit into his hand and applied a dab to each end of his black handlebar moustache. Just then, Heavy, the RTO, who sat at the end of the line monitoring the radio, spoke loudly enough to Drieser for Leon to hear.

"Higher wants us to search the village and then hump back to Tan Tru," Heavy said in that emotionless voice he used no matter what the message he happened to be relaying. He hung the handset back on the radio's shoulder strap, then went about finishing his breakfast.

Drieser received the news by giving his moustache another twist, and then he removed a laminated map from the leg pocket of his fatigues. He spread the map over his knees, and set to plotting the distance the squad had to go.

"Hear that, Preach? We're humping in," Leon said in disgust while lacing his rolled poncho to the bottom of his ruck. "Must be a hundred choppers sitting around doing nothing right this minute and we gotta hump." Leon paused and stared at Preacher with a pained look. "God, I hate this fucking place. When I get home, I ain't even going to walk in my sleep."

While Leon bitched, Monroe hopped onto the candy-stripe to retrieve the claymores he'd placed there the night before. It wasn't a two-man job, but as usual, Conroy followed his friend. After Monroe removed the blasting caps from the mines, Conroy wound a thin electrical cord neatly around the detonators and stuffed them back in their carrying bags. Conroy and Monroe were an odd pair, and none of the men—Monroe included—had ever completely understood their attraction to each other.

Conroy hailed from a little town by the name of Pearock, Kansas. Conroy said the town only had one road in or out, and claimed the water tower sported these words: Pearock. A Nice Place To Turn Around. None of the men believed him the night he first told about it—they'd all been drinking and Conroy was about two beers from puking—and he'd eventually written his father, asking him to take a picture of the tower and send it over. He now wore it tucked into the elastic band securing his camouflaged helmet cover. The picture had gotten wet so many times it was worthless to look at, but Conroy didn't care, he knew what it looked like.

Conroy joined the army the day he turned eighteen, and his voice, though it was a bit late in life for such things, hadn't finished changing. At times it sounded deep and normal enough, but more often than not it crackled with the pitch of boyhood. It was an endless source of embarrassment for him and he'd tried everything from throat lozenges to voice exercises to control it. Nothing helped. He could sing, though. He had a nice voice for that. Singing gave him control over the changes in pitch, and everyone considered him a fairly good singer. Monroe included, though he hated the country music Conroy enjoyed singing.

Norman Childers Monroe was born and raised in the Los Angeles ghetto of Watts. By some quirk in the way the Army assigned men to their units, Monroe wound up as 1st platoon's only black, a fact he complained about from time to time.

Most likely Monroe and Conroy would never have met back in the world, let alone hit it off, but here they became the best of friends. Conroy once admitted he'd never been more than a hundred miles from Pearock in his life. Monroe's street-smarts, and the stories he told of life in the ghetto, fascinated Conroy to no end. He could listen to Monroe for hours if his pal happened to be in a talkative mood.

For his part, Monroe appeared to accept Conroy's fawning with a bemused tolerance. Monroe understood Conroy was naive to the point of being harmless, and guessed the part of the country Conroy came from had to be so white that Conroy most likely couldn't even spell the word *nigger*, let alone ever have seen the need to use it.

In due time the men were saddled and Drieser had them on the candy-stripe and heading for the village. Leon took point and the rest of the men fell in behind him. By now the sun had broken through the cloud cover, burning away the night's damp chill. For a few meters the soldiers moved stiffly, gradually falling into that weary, slouched stride of men accustomed to walking for hours at a time.

Chapter 2

Monroe hated searching villages, and always had. So while the rest of the squad split up—Drieser and Heavy took one side of the village, Leon and Preacher the other—Monroe and Conroy took a position in the village center and secured the area.

Like always, the children of the village huddled around Monroe the moment they spotted him, touching the dark skin of his arms, and murmuring excitedly.

If the white soldiers and their long noses appeared strange, the color of Monroe's skin was downright unearthly. The children rubbed at it with nervous giggles and squeals. They pushed up his pant's legs and stroked his calves.

Monroe appeared to tolerate all this attention with indifference, though everyone knew he plainly enjoyed it. He liked kids no matter where he found them, and like children everywhere, they sensed this. Monroe missed his eight-year-old brother Lyman more than anyone else in his family. Being around these kids gave him a feeling of closeness to his brother, and he seldom passed up an opportunity to play with them when he could. He would select a boy close to Lyman's age and sit him on his lap, then break into a monologue, telling the wide-eyed boy his name, where he came from, what his girl-friend looked like, all to the befuddled amusement of the children watching.

Monroe kept his head shaved, and he wore the look well. He was over six feet tall with square shoulders that tapered to narrow hips. His face drew a cleft in its chin whenever he smiled. He was handsome and vain about his appearance. His fatigues never appeared as dirty as the other men's, and once in a while he'd even polish his worn-out boots.

If the children were intrigued with Monroe, the appearance of Conroy and his teeth sent them into screams of delight. "Beaucoup," several of the older ones murmured in awe while pointing at

Conroy's mouth.

Most everyone in the squad agreed Conroy was the homeliest person any of them had ever laid eyes on. His chin was shallow to the point of not being there, and he possessed a mouthful of buck teeth hanging so far from his face that, try as he might, his lips never seemed able to accommodate them. When he talked, he looked like he might be trying to spit a few of them out. His teeth were one of the reasons Conroy had enlisted in the first place. He'd been told by the recruiter that the Army would do something about them. He was still waiting. Conroy's eyes were large, dark, and set too close to each other over a stubby nose. Conroy looked like a rodent of some sort, and a number of the men tried for a while to hang that name on him. But Monroe would have nothing of it.

"Man that ugly got enough heartache as it is," Monroe said, the first time the idea came up. "Ain't no need to remind him."

The last hut on Leon and Preacher's side of the village belonged to Tuan's mother, and when they stepped inside, she was squatting beside a rice pot, stirring it with a long wooden spoon.

In one corner of the hootch sat a low, two-shelved shrine. On the top shelf an old framed photo of her father and mother leaned among sticks of incense poking from mud holders. On the second shelf sat Tuan's gift.

"My old man would go nuts if he could see this," Preacher said, bending forward for a better look at the shrine. "Did ya know some of these people worship their ancestors?"

"I guess," Leon said absently. He'd been five wet days without his boots off, and his feet hurt something terrible. Even the calluses would be soft and flaky by this time. He hoped again Drieser might finagle some way of arranging for a chopper to pick them up. Just thinking about the long walk home depressed him.

Preacher glanced over his shoulder to see if the woman was watching, then reached for Tuan's gift, still wrapped in its grass bow. He untied it carefully, then turned to Leon, who continued watching Tuan's mother fiddle with the rice pot because there wasn't anything else in the place to hold his attention.

Preacher hurried across the room. "Smell this," he said, handing the box to Leon.

Leon pulled off the lid and stared down at the brown beans.
"Smells like vanilla, don't it?" Preach said.

At first Leon hadn't been able to place the smell. "Yeah," he
nodded, taking another whiff. "Where do you suppose it came
from?" he said, going to the table and placing the box there. He
removed a bean, rolling it between his fingers.

Just then, Monroe and Conroy stepped through the doorway.

"What are you two fools doing in here so long?" Monroe said.
"It'll be dark by the time we get back the way you in here fucking
around."

"Smell this, Monroe," Leon said, holding out the bean. "It's like
vanilla or something."

Monroe sauntered forward and took the bean from him. "What
you mean like? This is vanilla."

He dropped heavily into one of the chairs at the table. "Vanilla
planifolia, if you want to get technical," he said, rummaging a finger in the box. "My old man would gladly give his left testicle to be
able to grow this shit back home."

"Smells like a bakery," Conroy said, managing to say a complete
sentence like an adult.

"Pop would say it smells like money," Monroe laughed. He tossed
the bean in the box and stood up. "Come on. Let's book."

"How's it smell like money?" Preacher asked, once everyone
was outside and walking back through the village. He'd palmed
one of the beans when no one was looking and waved it beneath
his nose.

"My pop has been trying to grow that shit ever since I can
remember. He got so many pots hanging from the balcony of our
apartment it look like a greenhouse back there. My mother thinks
he's crazy, but he don't pay her no mind. Just keeps telling her one
a these fine days he's gonna figure out how to grow the shit, and
she'll think different."

"You mean he's trying to grow vanilla?" Leon said.

Monroe lit a Salem, and blew the smoke over his shoulder. "No.
He's trying to grow the orchid. He get that done, he'll have the
vanilla."

Leon jogged a few steps and closed the distance between them.
"That's where vanilla comes from? Orchids?"

Monroe shot Leon a sideways glance, chuckling. "Where you

think it come from?"

"Guess I never thought about it," Leon said, and after a time: "Why's your dad want to grow it? Can't he just go to the store and buy it?"

At this, Monroe stopped short and faced Leon. "He don't wanna eat the shit. He wants to make money with it." Monroe looked from Leon out into the paddies. His face grew tight about the lips, then softened at the possibility. "He could, too, if he had the land and the damn things would grow for him."

Up ahead, Drieser and Heavy exited the farthest hut at the other end of the village. Drieser pressed the radio's handset to his ear while Heavy waited at his side. Leon watched and prayed the call was for a lift back to base camp.

Monroe took the scene in with a glance and shifted the ruck on his back. "The second night of the Watts riots, Pop loaded me in the car and we headed out. I figured I knew what he was up to. Everybody else was out in the streets looting and shit and I guessed we was going to get our share. But not him. You know what that man did?" Monroe's face broke a tired smile, and his head shook at the memory. "He pulled in behind a greenhouse and busted a window out with a tire iron and we went in and stole all the orchids."

Smoke rushed from Monroe's nostrils. "Can you believe that shit?" he said, looking from one man to the other. "All my buddies are getting new TVs and stuff, and here me an' Pop are stealing flowers."

"Hey, that's neat," Conroy said, always ready to believe that anything connected with Monroe must surely have been important.

"NEAT!" Monroe snapped, throwing the cigarette down and grinding it into the thin layer of mud. "How neat you think it be when my friends are asking me what I took an' I gotta tell them we cleaned all the orchids from a greenhouse?"

The approach of Drieser and Heavy changed the subject. Heavy tottered a few blind steps behind, trying to clean the lenses of his glasses on the tail of his fatigue shirt. Before reaching the men, Drieser pointed back the other way.

"Leon. Ya'll take the point," he drawled. "Keep to the dikes best you can. The rest of you know the drill. Let's move out."

Chapter 3

That same morning, Tucker Burdick watched from the open porthole of a Chinook helicopter making its descent into the 2/60th's base camp at Tan Tru. Tucker peeked at his watch—0530—then down at the shadowed green paddies passing below.

The tattoo he'd gotten two drunken nights ago in Manila on the last night of his R&R itched. He popped open the top button of his fatigue shirt and stared down at the black ink outline of a flintlock rifle lying across an oak leaf laurel. He now had a permanent Combat Infantry Badge above his left nipple. And though he'd always been proud of what the badge stood for—only the infantry received it, and only after being in combat—for the first time it struck him that he was going to wear it for the rest of his life, and he wasn't quite sure how he felt about the idea. On the ground, where even a minor wound often turned into a festering sore, he'd be lucky if it didn't become infected.

He craved a smoke, but this was out of the question. Pallets of ammunition were stacked so high in the cargo bay of the Chinook he couldn't see over them. Tucker guessed if all that ordnance were to go off at once it would most likely leave a permanent hole in the sky. He imagined chunks of himself flying through the air at the outer edge of a burst of white light.

He'd been able to hitch a ride on this re-supply chopper after sharing a couple of beers with its crew chief, who he'd met on the return flight from Manila.

By 0500 that morning they were in the air, and after a brief stop at 9th Division headquarters at Dong Tam, were about to land outside the 2/60th's base camp at Tan Tru.

Good light was still a few minutes away, but with the lift-ship continuing its descent, Tucker could make out the canvas roofed buildings situated every which way inside the perimeter wire as much by happenchance as anything.

Down there, the base camp circled around an oval-shaped mound of dry paddy mud bordered on one side by the village of Tan Tru. On the other, like a strand of caramel ribbon, the Song Vam Co Tay wound toward the South China Sea. The perimeter of the camp was double rows of concertina wire running outside evenly spaced khaki-colored sandbag bunkers.

The pilot maneuvered the Chinook into a slow backward hover on the road near the camp's main gate. Tucker jerked his face from the window when grit and dust from the road were sucked in the open porthole, and the chopper touched down with a heavy bounce. In another minute the cargo door opened with a whine of hydraulics. The crew chief, a pot bellied lifer whose name Tucker never did learn, gave him a grinning thumbs-up, and Tucker waved back, then squeezed past the crates and down to the road, hurrying away from the rotor wash, and the blast of the Chinook's engines.

Tucker had only been gone a week, but the entire time he'd been unable to shake the uncomfortable feeling that R&R was somewhere he didn't belong. His first night in Manila he'd been afraid to leave his hotel room. For the first time in ten months he'd understood he was safe. But he felt naked, vulnerable. The bustle of traffic in the streets, the carrying-on of everyday life confused him. Six hours away his friends were sweating out another uncomfortable night in the Nam, and here he was, safe, a pocket full of money, and wishing he were with them.

But that was then. Now he was...what, home? Tucker laughed at the thought and picked up his flight-bag. "Yeah, you stupid ass," he said, moving for the gate. "You're home."

On the other side of the wire a jeep waited, engine idling. Two men were kicked back on its seats, their bare arms tan beneath green flak vests. One man wore a pair of aviator sunglasses while reading a crumpled magazine. The other smoked a cigarette and itched a hand back and forth over the top of his head. To the right was a twenty-foot guard tower, one man in the top of it silhouetted by the low clouds. He had his shirt off, gazing at something far down the road.

In the center of the camp, surrounded by a sandbag revetment, Tucker passed the diesel generator, which hammered so steadily the soldiers only noticed its sound when it was down for repairs. A few buildings away the cooks were preparing breakfast, and the doors on refrigerated boxes behind the mess hall slammed shut with drum-like thumps. The guys over in artillery shouted and repeated fire mission coordinates, while breaches were loaded and slapped shut on the 155's. A serious sound, that locking and loading of the big guns: heavy brass sliding into steel barrels with precise metallic clicks.

Tucker rounded a curve on the worn path and Charlie Company's CQ shack came in view: a sandbagged Quonset hut on the far end of the area. The rest of the camp's buildings were square, wood-sided affairs, with screens that started at waist level and rose to canvas roofs. The screens were of little use since most had gaping holes, and none of the hootches were fitted with doors. To guard against flooding, all the structures sat atop rusting, fifty-five gallon drums.

As soon as Tucker entered the company area, he heard a transistor radio playing in 2nd platoon's hootch, the Armed Forces Network weatherman in Saigon delivering the day's forecast in an excited tone of voice. Why anyone cared what the weather would be like, Tucker didn't understand. Could it matter? The forecast might just as well be given once and never mentioned again: "It's going to be a hot year. If the sun ain't shining, you can bet it's going to rain. And there's no change in sight."

Just then an anonymous voice yelled from inside 2nd platoon's hootch: "How was the R&R, Lucky?"

Tucker stopped and looked, but couldn't see beyond the shadowy screens.

"Real drunk," he lied, and kept moving. He had gotten drunk, but only one night, with the tattoo being the result. Tucker knew by the way the man had called him Lucky it wasn't anyone he cared to stop and chat about his R&R with. None of his friends used the nickname because they knew he hated it. Lucky? Luck was something that ran out.

He did allow he'd been lucky, and luck was all it amounted to. It embarrassed him, the fuss everyone made over the fact that his helmet had once been shot off his head three times in the same day.

Tucker and his best friend Leon were once pinned down for an hour behind a paddy dike by a well-sighted sniper in a treeline a good hundred meters away. Any time they moved, rounds struck the top of the dike, spraying them with chunks of baked mud.

After the first shot, Leon stayed put and waited for help to arrive, but for some reason Tucker kept looking up to get a fix on the sniper, and each time he did, a well placed round knocked the helmet from his head. Three times this happened. And three times, Tucker retrieved it as calmly as if it were a wind-blown hat, examined the hole, and put the helmet back in place.

Word of the incident spread until the helmet took on a talismanic quality. Men slapped the helmet for luck when they leapt from hovering choppers. If the platoon worked with the Riverine Forces, the soldiers wanted Tucker to wait by the open door of the landing craft so they might touch the helmet when they filed past.

Eventually the whole affair turned into such a nuisance that Tucker set the helmet on a wood fence post outside 1st platoon's hootch. And superstition or not, even the skeptics among them couldn't resist touching it when they passed.

Located on the other side of path where Tucker walked was the company's three-hole latrine. Tucker stopped short when from the corner of his eye he saw something there.

On the screen door was a curiosity he'd heard about, but had never seen before. Now and then Higgins, the company clerk, would show up at the hootch, carrying on about some shithouse fly. Higgins claimed the thing spent its days crawling over the waste tubs beneath the latrine until it had grown to the size of a small bird.

Higgins may have exaggerated the size of the shithouse fly a bit, but Tucker had to admit the one in front of him now was the largest he'd ever seen. The fly was round enough to cover a quarter and solid black. Its wings looked small in proportion to its body, and Tucker figured it had grown so plump from eating shit that its wings couldn't hold it in the air for long. He took a few cautious steps forward and pulled a Zippo from his pants pocket. When he touched the flame to the screen, the fly sprang from its resting spot with a drooping flight and hovered for one unsteady moment above the bench, then tumbled out of sight through the hole below.

Tucker waited, hoping the fly would make another appearance. When it didn't, he guessed the fat thing was where it wanted to be, and continued on for the hootch.

When he arrived the place was empty, and Tucker stood in the middle of the hootch re-acquainting himself with its unique odor. It smelled of sweat, dampness, and flourishing mildew, a ripeness that always reminded him of rotting apples. Tucker's boots scuffed grit over the floor until he stood beside his cot. There happened to be a letter lying on it, his father's large scrawl plainly visible on the envelope even from a few feet away.

A sudden, sharp pain in his bowels made him grimace. His R&R diet of steaks each night for supper had bound him up tighter than a new catcher's mitt. He figured he'd better head for the latrine and make an effort to unclog himself. If nothing else, the latrine was a good place to read his father's letter.

A few meters behind the latrine, the camp's Vietnamese barber paced outside his half of the building he shared with Tay Ninh's Laundry. In the barber's hand, a palm frond broom created a haze of red dust at his feet. The rustle of the fronds sounded out of place to Tucker's ear, like the soft scraping of maples leaves, the wind brushing them over the clapboard siding of his father's house, back home in Teal, the small Iowa town where he and his best friend Leon were from.

Tucker guessed his father was there right this minute, drunk enough by now to dull the stench of the chicken innards he waded through each day in the gut pit at Hansel Bros. Poultry. Despite the foul odor clinging to the air around the latrine, Tucker could recall the stench of the plant and the redolent smell of shit and dead chickens that over the years seemed to have saturated the outer layer of his father's skin.

Tucker had worked in the plant, too. His dad got him the job right after he'd graduated from high school. The first time he spotted his father in the pit, waist deep in the purple-gray guts, his chest waders coated with slime, Tucker backed away from the sight so quickly he nearly stepped in front of a forklift.

"Get used to it," his father said, staring up at him with puffy red eyes.

At that moment Tucker promised himself he'd never stick around long enough to get used to any of it.

Tucker let the latrine door slam behind him when he stepped in. The flies resting on the screens encircling the place began to buzz every which way through the narrow room before landing again.

At the farthest hole, Tucker unfastened his pants and let them fall to his ankles. After adjusting himself as comfortably as possible on the rough-cut wood, he opened his father's letter.

Chapter 4

Eighty meters away, First Sergeant Boyle—Top, to everyone in the company—was entering the CQ shack for another day at the office.

The CQ was the only Quonset hut in the base camp. The hut was thirty feet long, fifteen feet across, and housed Charlie Company's headquarters staff. The place had arched corrugated iron walls and was divided into three sections. The company clerk, PFC Higgins' desk faced the entryway. To the left was Captain Decker's office, the company commander. To the right, Boyle's.

The hut was encased in a layer of sandbags faded to a cream-like color under the intense delta sun. With the sun shining on it—and it seemed the sun was always shining—the CQ could be seen from a good distance out in the surrounding paddies. Even at night, if there happened to be a decent moon, the building stood out. After the first time Captain Decker viewed the CQ at night, the way it appeared to be a luminous whale resting just inside the wire, he had commissioned Higgins to make a sign to hang over the building's entryway. Painted in red block letters on a plank taken from the side of an artillery round case were a few words from Melville: WONDER YE THEN AT THE FIERY HUNT? Later on, someone had painted a C over the H, and despite a half-hearted attempt by Boyle to find the culprit, no one had ever gotten around to making it right again.

When Boyle stepped in his doorway the first thing he saw was Bastard, 1st platoon's Japanese Macaque monkey, who had wandered in sometime during the night. From the looks of the place, Bastard hadn't come in there to sleep. Papers and file jackets had been torn and scattered about the room. Drawers of the desk and file cabinet sitting behind it hung open. There were even a few small piles of Bastard's droppings here and there on the floor. But Boyle didn't pay much attention to any of this, because Bastard was sitting on the desk, one hand moving quickly between his outstretched legs, masturbating.

On more than one occasion Boyle had threatened to kill Bastard. The men knew this and tried to keep Bastard on a chain attached to a bunker behind their hootch. But someone was forever setting him loose, and most of the time Bastard roamed freely about the company area, looking for handouts, and getting into places he wasn't welcome.

In fact, none of the men in the platoon liked the monkey much. Bastard was nearly as wild as the day he was born, and though none of them would admit to it, most were afraid to go near him. Despite his small size—he was only a little over two feet tall—all the men agreed he was a fearsome sight when angry: the hair on top of his bullet-shaped head bristling, his lips drawn back to show long canine teeth. About the only time he allowed anyone within arm's reach was if handouts were forthcoming. He ate most anything, C-ration cookies especially. He could be pleasant enough if he smelled them in someone's pocket or hand, and would allow whoever had them to pet him while he ate. But all things considered, he made a poor pet. The men tolerated him only because he'd belonged to Pearl, and Pearl was dead. Somehow it didn't seem right for them to get rid of his monkey.

If Bastard felt any fear at seeing Boyle frozen in the doorway like an Easter Island carving just then, it didn't show. His fingers continued moving between his legs like he happened to be the only one in the room, a button-sized drop of semen dribbled onto the desk.

There was a .45 automatic holstered on Boyle's right hip, and when Boyle unsnapped the holster, Bastard heard the sound and looked hard at him.

"By God, that's just about the limit," Boyle said, leveling the gun.

Bastard had been around long enough to recognize the object in Boyle's hand as something loud, but at the moment there wasn't anywhere to run. He rose to his hind legs, sniffed the air, and waited for Boyle to make the next move.

Boyle could feel sweat beading beneath his thinning red hair, between his shoulder blades, and under his arms. Soon it would all collect around his ample waist, soaking the band of his fatigue pants, causing him more discomfort than just about anything he could think of.

Boyle had never been able to hit much with a .45, and he didn't know of anyone who could. Coupled with this was the fact he'd gotten drunk again the night before, falling on his shooting arm when he'd staggered outside to puke. It pained him a good deal just to raise the gun, let alone hold it steady enough to aim. So when his first shot missed by a foot and blew a dime-sized hole in the file cabinet, he wasn't surprised.

The second shot missed even farther than the first, for by now, Bastard had taken to running around the room, screeching, and becoming more frightened with each lap.

The only escape was the doorway and Boyle had that blocked off. Each time Bastard made a move in that direction, Boyle's boot would kick at him.

Boyle squeezed off a third shot just as Bastard leaped from the desk to the file cabinet. There was a picture of Boyle's soon-to-be-ex-wife hanging on the wall, and the slug hit it dead center. The glass shattered, and the photo looked for a moment like it might fall, but stayed put. Gloria stared back at him with a round gap in her smile.

"You lousy bitch," Boyle said under his breath, and for a moment thought about seeing if he might not be able to hit her again. Instead, he pointed and fired just as Bastard ducked behind the desk.

The round passed through the left front leg of the desk, splintering it. The desk teetered for a moment, then tipped to a side-heavy angle, and a pen and pencil set slid to the plank floor.

In an instant Boyle charged to the desk, and dropping to his knees, stared in at Bastard, who had backed into the leg space beneath it.

"Your ass is mine now, motherfucker!" Boyle said, attempting to draw a bead on Bastard, who kept a steady chatter going while bouncing from one side to the other.

Boyle was afraid that even at this distance he might miss in the darkness below the desk, so he did the one thing he shouldn't have: he reached in and attempted to grab Bastard by the throat.

And Bastard did the only thing he could. He grabbed Boyle's hand in both of his and sank his teeth into the webbing between the index and thumb. When Boyle jerked his hand back, Bastard was attached to it: his arms, legs, and tail wrapped tightly around the forearm.

About this time, Higgins, Boyle's favorite drinking partner, stepped in the doorway of the CQ. It had been Higgins' foot that caused Boyle to trip the night before. The two of them had been having a high time of it, drinking and playing cribbage in Boyle's quarters, when Boyle suddenly went quiet and staggered to his feet. Higgins was only trying to make way for him when their feet became tangled, sending Boyle's shoulder onto the corner of his footlocker.

The first thing Higgins noticed upon entering the CQ was a film of blue smoke drifting from the doorway of Boyle's office and into his own. For a moment he thought he might be seeing things. He had a world-class hangover, and the fat joint he'd smoked before showing up for work was causing everything to appear a bit hazy. But there wasn't anything wrong with his nose, and the potent smell of cordite hung heavy enough in the air that, stoned or not, he was afraid Boyle had followed through on his threat to kill himself after receiving Gloria's Dear John letter a few days before.

But not only was Boyle alive, he had something large on his arm that he was playing around with.

When Boyle saw Higgins watching him, he stopped his gyrations and screamed at him.

"Bastard!"

Higgins let out a whoop. "Way to go, Top!" he laughed, slapping his hands together happily. "You finally caught him!"

"Bastard!" Boyle screamed again, the pain in his hand making it difficult for him to say even that much.

"He is that, Top."

Bastard wasn't showing any signs of letting go. All the spinning around Boyle had been doing made him dizzy. Since Boyle's arm was about the only thing at the moment he was sure of, he clung to it tightly, bitting harder each time Boyle shook.

"Goddamn it, Higgins! I need help!"

It dawned on Higgins the trickle of blood he could see running down Boyle's arm might not be Bastard's. "Top! You're bleeding!"

Boyle hurried back to where he'd dropped the .45 when Bastard first attacked. With some effort, he knelt and retrieved the gun.

"Now I got you," Boyle said, raising his arm for a clear shot.

"Not in here, Top!" Higgins said, covering his ears.

"Hold still, damn it," Boyle muttered, attempting to force the .45 into the side of Bastard's head.

Naturally, seeing the object so close to his face only increased Bastard's fear, with the result of making him struggle all the harder.

"Fire in the hole!" Higgins yelled, plugging his ears and ducking just as Boyle pulled the trigger.

The round only grazed the tip of Bastard's ear, blowing a clock off the wall on the other side of the room.

For a moment Boyle forgot the pain in his hand, and stared with a dumbfounded expression at the gun. Bastard took this opportunity to release Boyle's arm. Before either Boyle or Higgins could react, Bastard darted between Higgins' legs and out of the office.

Boyle was too concerned with his damaged hand to give chase: not that he could have nabbed Bastard anyway. Nobody could if he didn't want to be caught.

Holding his injured hand with the other, Boyle spread back his thumb for Higgins to inspect. "How bad is it?" he said.

Higgins stood a head taller than Boyle and wore bifocals. He leaned forward, bobbing his face, adjusting the angle of the dirty lenses resting on the middle of his long nose. During their drinking session the night before, Boyle had sprayed Higgins' face with foam when he'd opened a warm can of Falstaff. At the time, Higgins had been too drunk and stoned to clean them, so now it appeared as if small bubbles were floating in front of him. For a moment Higgins let the dope take over and forgot what he was supposed to be looking at.

"Higgins!"

"Yeah, Top?"

"My hand," Boyle said as evenly as he could under the circumstances. He knew Higgins spent his days stoned as a rock, but as long as the company ran well enough to keep Captain Decker off his back, and as long as Higgins would drink and lose money playing cribbage with him at night, he didn't care if the man was in a coma.

With all the blood, it was tough to tell, but Higgins could clearly see the outline of Bastard's teeth. There were also two evenly spaced gashes where the canines had torn the skin. Actually, all the bleeding Boyle had been doing made the bite look worse than it was.

"Don't look so bad to me, Top."

Boyle drew his hand back and looked for himself. "You saw it, Higgins. That ape tried to eat me." He lowered himself into the Naugahyde visitor's chair in the corner and immediately wished he hadn't. His fatigue shirt was soaked with sweat and the chair's vinyl covering caused it to stick to his back like flypaper. He leaned forward and cradled his hand while studying the bloody outline of Bastard's teeth on his skin.

"That monkey's a goddamn menace, Higgins. I want it dead. ASAP."

"We can't, Top."

"Who the hell does the fucker belong to anyway? I'm gonna see he gets an Article-15."

"He don't belong to nobody, Top. He just hangs around over at first platoon's hootch. He's like their mascot."

"So what? Pick a man and tell him to shoot that monkey!"

"We best not do that, Top."

Boyle's hand started to throb: his arm ached clear to the elbow. "And why the hell not?"

"Captain Decker likes him. He thinks Bastard's good for morale."

"Morale! Free pussy would be good for morale." Boyle stared at his hand for a long thoughtful moment. "Then have someone discipline him."

"Discipline him, Top?"

"Yes, discipline!" Boyle barked, wincing as he stood up. "Give him a good beating or something, I don't know. But I want that little asshole brought back in line."

"Right, Top. I'll have him disciplined."

"And do something about that desk before the captain sees it. I'm going over to the aid-station. Fucker's probably given me rabies."

"Don't you worry, Top. I'll take care of it. Go get yourself patched up."

As soon as Boyle was gone, Higgins went to his own desk and sat down. He stretched his long legs over it, leaned back, and rotated his head while the spots on his lenses caught the light from a bare bulb hanging from the ceiling. It produced a kaleidoscope-like effect he found fascinating.

Chapter 5

Tucker had long since given up his business in the latrine, and was presently sitting on his cot, because he couldn't think of anything else to do. Once Top spotted him loafing around he'd soon find something to keep him busy, so he planned on hiding out for a while longer if he could.

While Tucker sat in the latrine reading his father's letter, he had heard gunfire, but thought little of it. From the muffled sound of the shots, Tucker figured most likely one of the bunker guards was thinning the ranks of the rat population inside his bunker. Of course indiscriminate firing of weapons was against regulations, but like the saying went: "What are they gonna do, send me to Vietnam?"

The letter from his father, as always, left Tucker feeling more alone than ever. The man wrote the same way in which he carried on all conversations. Just once Tucker would have liked to hear about something other than the long list of grievances his father had with Hansel Bros. Poultry, and the *cocksuckers* who ran it. Tucker couldn't recall hearing his father talk about the place without using that word, and it appeared he couldn't write without it either.

He suddenly felt hungry, and knew if he wanted something other than C's for breakfast he would need to hurry.

Tucker had only taken a few steps away from the hootch when he looked up and saw Boyle bearing down on him from the direction of the aid-station: one bloody hand held forward like a guidon.

Tucker jogged to the latrine and ducked inside. He snatched the letter from the pocket of his fatigues, then hurriedly dropped them once more and sat on the farthest hole, pretending to read. Maybe Top would be too occupied with whatever happened to his hand to notice him. No such luck.

"Burdick. Is that you?" Top yelled from a short distance away, dipping his head, trying to see past the rusty screens.

"Yeah, Top," Tucker answered, putting a friendly tone to his voice he didn't feel.

An instant later, Boyle entered the place. He unfastened his pants below the gun belt, letting them fall the way Tucker had. The .45 stayed on his hip.

"Rear echelon motherfuckers," Boyle said, adding a loud fart for punctuation. "Did you know the aid-station don't open until eight?"

Tucker didn't think Boyle was actually expecting an answer so he kept quiet. Besides, having anyone on the hole next to him was not something Tucker enjoyed, and if there was one person he didn't want to share the latrine with that morning, it was Boyle. Most times the man talked just to hear himself.

"Somebody oughta tell them assholes there's a war going on," Boyle said, and he held his wounded hand in the air for Tucker's benefit.

Tucker tried his best to appear interested in the letter. He shot Boyle a sideways glance, and nodded his head absently. Several minutes passed before Boyle spoke again.

"Letter from home?" he said, as if it could have come from somewhere else.

Tucker nodded.

"Last letter I got my wife said she was filing for a divorce," Boyle said.

Tucker raised himself with both hands and took a new, more comfortable position on the coarse seat.

"We was only married a couple years," Boyle went on—as Tucker knew he would. "She could of at least waited till I got home. Don't you think?"

"I wouldn't know, Top," Tucker said.

"Yeah," Boyle sighed. "A real bitch, that one."

Tucker folded the letter into his chest pocket. Boyle was in a chatty mood and there would be little use pretending to read a letter he hadn't wanted to read once, let alone twice.

"You married, Burdick?"

"No."

"Stay that way," Boyle said.

"Why'd you marry her if she was such a bitch, Top?"

"Let me tell you something, son," Boyle said. "Ain't but one thing running this world. Pussy. Men will fight and die for it. Spend all their money on it, and chase it till they can't run no more. You following me?"

"I guess."

"Gloria was my third wife, and you can damn well bet she won't be my last." Boyle produced another crisp fart. "A whiskey glass and a woman's ass will make a fool out of any man, Burdick. Take it from me, son. Poon. Now that's where the real power in this world is. You ever start thinking different, you come and see Cleo Boyle."

Tucker didn't care to hear any more of Boyle's shithouse musings. A fly buzzed his ear and he took a swipe at it. There was a loud plop from below Boyle's end of the latrine, followed by a groan of relief, and several flies hurried up through the vacant hole between: The shithouse fly among them. The fat thing plopped onto the wood next to Boyle and stayed put.

"Where in Texas you from, anyway, Burdick?"

"I'm from, Iowa, Top," Tucker said. The fly began inching toward Boyle's bare ass.

"Can't say as I ever been there."

"Lot of people haven't," Tucker said.

"You like it there?"

"Not much. Better than here, I guess."

"Now, ain't that the truth," Boyle said and stared down at his hand. He wished there was someone he could have a drink with. What the hell, he'd have one with himself when he was finished.

"You're in first platoon, ain't you Burdick?"

"Yeah," Tucker said. A number of flies had now gathered at Boyle's end of the latrine.

"Who owns that monkey?" Boyle asked.

"Bastard?"

"We got more than one monkey running around here, Burdick?"

"He's the only one I know about, Top."

A couple of flies made a pass at Boyle's face and he waved his good arm at them. "So he's not your pet. Am I right?"

"Don't belong to me, Top."

"Good. Then you won't mind beating the piss out of him!"

The shithouse fly was nearly to Boyle's right cheek, and Tucker found it more interesting than Boyle's chit-chat.

"The son of a bitch attacked me this morning." Boyle nodded at his hand. Several more flies joined the others circling his head. He took a swat at one that tried landing on his face.

At this, Tucker swung his gaze to Boyle's hand, looking at it with interest for the first time. "Bastard really jumped you, Top?"

"Look at my hand."

"I don't think he's ever done that before," Tucker said. A few more flies rose from the hole and headed for Boyle's half of the latrine.

"Never mind that. He did it this time." Boyle said. He was waving both arms in front of his face, now.

"I could see it if he was a dog or something, you know," Tucker said. "But a little—"

"Goddamn it, Burdick! Are you going to do something about that monkey or not?"

By now the flies were agitated. They buzzed loudly and struck the screening beside Boyle with soft thuds.

"I don't think I want to beat him, Top," Tucker said. "He never done nothing to me." Tucker hopped down and pulled up his pants. In two strides he was outside the latrine and looking back in at Boyle. From where he stood he could see the shithouse fly give a little leap and land on the bare skin of Boyle's rump.

"Goddamn these things!" Boyle said, swinging at the flies around his head with both hands like a boxer working a speed bag.

"You never answered my question, Top. Why'd you marry her if she was such a bitch?" Tucker said. He couldn't believe the man didn't feel the huge insect on his skin.

"I already told you why. Now this is a direct order, Burdick. Beat that fucking monkey, or else!"

Tucker wasn't afraid of Boyle or his constant threats. And besides, everyone knew Boyle for a blowhard slacker who ran the loosest company in the battalion. Boyle never followed up on anything. Tucker pulled a Marlboro from behind his ear and lit it. "You know you can't give me a direct order, Top."

Boyle's pale complexion turned a fine pink. He jerked his face from side to side and blew at the flies.

"I'll have you busted for insubordination!"

"I can't go much lower than I am, Top," Tucker said, motioning at the single chevron and rocker on his sleeve. By the expression on Boyle's face, Tucker figured he was close to assigning him to a day's duty manning one of the observation posts along the road that ran from the camp to Highway 4. Tucker hoped so. The OPs were safe, and more of a day off than anything, but Boyle, for some reason no one understood, thought them a form of punishment.

"We'll see about that!" Boyle snapped.

It seemed that now every fly in the place had been attracted to Boyle. Swarming like they were feeding on a carcass, the flies landed on his legs, his face, some were attracted to the blood on his arm. He reached for the toilet paper but there wasn't any: only an empty tube hanging on the holder next to him. When he looked up, Tucker was grinning around the cigarette.

By now the flies were unbearable. Boyle looked to the other wall, the TP holder there empty as well. He jumped off the hole and dropped down to pull up his fatigues, and when he did, the shithouse fly inched around the side of Boyle's right cheek and from the corner of his eye he got a glimpse of it for the first time.

Boyle screamed, jerking upright and forward so suddenly his face mashed into the screen. He danced around, swatting his bare butt as if he'd been scalded, the holster clapping his leg like a deformed third hand. He turned in time to see the fly circle the hole once and drop into it.

Boyle peeked cautiously down the hole, then bent quickly to pull up his pants. "Holy shit, Burdick," Boyle muttered. "Did you see the size of that—?" But Tucker was already on his way to the mess hall. Boyle's foot kicked the screen door open and he charged from the latrine. He fumbled beneath his belly and gun belt for the button of his pants. "Burn these tubs when you get back, Burdick!" Boyle hollered. "And put some fucking paper in this place! Just once I'd like to come in here and be able to wipe my ass when I'm done! Hear me?"

Tucker waved an arm over his shoulder and flipped the cigarette in a high arc.

Boyle stomped away in the other direction, mumbling to himself about the indignity of it all, and wanting a drink more than ever.

The flies buzzed back down the holes to see what was new.

Chapter 6

By keeping to the dikes the squad covered just over three kilometers in the last forty-five minutes. It was raining off and on the entire time. Leon led the men in a zigzagging march over the dikes, keeping due east by way of north or south, before catching a dike running east again. Of course the shortest way would have been to just cut straight through the paddies themselves, but this would have meant wadding in knee-deep water and calf-high mud that pulled at boots like peanut butter.

The men were relaxed, but cautious. They felt fairly secure since the Plain of Reeds was behind them, and the nearest treeline was a good three-hundred meters distant, which was within mortar range, of course, but too far out for an ambush.

The rain let up again, leaving a thick cover of dirty gray clouds blocking the heat of the morning sun, and the soldiers were in a good mood, knowing home waited at the end of their march.

Four meters behind Leon, Monroe walked the slack position. Now and then Leon picked up the tune Monroe sang quietly to himself, and even sang along softly when Monroe came to the only words of the song Leon knew—I'm a soul man—all the while keeping his eyes strained a short distance on the dike ahead, searching for anything there that might appear out of the ordinary. The dikes were difficult to booby-trap in the open, but it didn't mean Charlie Cong wouldn't try. Whenever Leon came upon a dip in one of the dikes, a depression that might signal the settling of dirt around something buried there, or anything that looked out of place, he stepped from the dike and led the squad in a wide arc through the paddy before climbing back to the dike and picking up the pace once more.

"Hey, Preach," Monroe called over his shoulder.

Preacher called back from his position a man behind. Conroy was following Monroe. Heavy chugged along behind Preacher, and

Sergeant Drieser walked drag.

"You still got that vanilla bean, ain't you?" Monroe asked.

Preacher felt in his shirt pocket before answering. "Affirmative."

"Don't let it go. I been thinking maybe I should send it to my ole man. He'll go ape-shit for sure." Monroe felt like talking. He fired a Salem, and let the cigarette dangle from his lips while he spoke. "When he found out I was coming here, he got all excited. You'd have thought I was heading out on some nature hike instead a this bad-ass place."

Monroe's voice dropped an octave like it always did whenever he imitated his father. "'Now, Monroe,' he says to me. 'You be sure an' keep your ass on the lookout for orchids, ya hear?'" Monroe puffed a cloud of blue smoke that hung in the still morning air until Conroy passed through it.

"Like I wasn't gonna have enough shit to watch out for. I ain't even gonna write a letter with it. Just send him the bean." Monroe chuckled at the thought. "That oughta drive his ass up the wall. Serve him right."

Leon joined in the conversation, but kept his eyes on the business at hand. "Think he could grow orchids from it, Monroe?"

"Who knows," Monroe said, shrugging beneath the shoulder straps of his ruck. "They ain't like planting petunias, ya know. Vanilla orchids will only grow in certain climates. Twenty-five degrees above or below the equator. L.A.'s about ten degrees too far north, but that don't keep the old boy from trying. He's hard-headed for sure. I give him that. Twenty years of work and the only vanilla that man ever smell come when my mother baking cookies. Ain't that some shit?"

"For sure," Conroy squeaked behind him. Embarrassed by the sound he made, he cleared his throat and fell silent.

"But you said if he had the land he could do it," Preacher said, and shifted the weight of the M-60 machine gun over to his left shoulder for a spell.

"That's a fact. Mexico. Now that's where the man should be. Me an' him drove down there once to check it out, too. Spent damn near a week looking around. The old man figured we could swing it if he had a stake. He knew that was near impossible, but even that woulda been easier than talking my mother into moving to Mexico. She said if he needed to hang out with Mexicans, he could haul his ass over to East L.A. any time he felt the urge. She wanted no part of it, so he's pretty much given up on the idea. Can't take the dream away from him though."

Monroe's voice trailed off, leaving the air filled with the sound of wet boots and the sporadic rattle of equipment being re-adjusted.

Up ahead the treelines were narrowing, closing off the paddies. The squad had no choice but to pass through in order to reach the open paddies on the other side. The bull session ended, while each of the men assumed an alertness that only moments before hadn't been there. Thumbs checked safeties of their rifles in reflex. Eyes scanned the trees ahead warily. Without a word spoken each man widened the distance between himself and the man in front.

The pace slowed considerably. Leon kept one eye on the dike, the other on the approaching treeline. He looked for an opening in the foliage ahead. One of the VC's favorite tricks was to lure sloppy troops into an ambush by putting out the welcome mat. A trail inviting quick access through the nipa palm was risky, and Leon always avoided them if at all possible.

A little over fifty meters from the edge of the left treeline, Leon brought everyone to a halt. There wasn't any good way to approach a treeline from the paddies. The men were easy targets for anyone lying in wait, but they didn't have much choice. At some point they had to cross. With open paddies behind, the only direction to go, if the treeline suddenly sprouted green tracers, was forward. The men took crouching positions, each facing left and right, ready to spread on line and dash into the nipa palm.

A gust of wind sifted through the trees and Leon reacted by sniffing the passing air. There were instances when it was possible to actually smell trouble. Leon had witnessed this himself. A guy named Rabbit had been able to do it. The men called him Rabbit because of the way his nose bounced in a permanent twitch after walking up on a well-concealed bunker and the muzzle of an AK-47 dry-fired into his stomach. Rabbit, once the best point man in the platoon, had kept the men from walking dead into an ambush one night when he'd detected the smell of unwashed armpits wafting on the night breeze. Leon had only been able to smell his own sour body odor that night, and it was all he could smell now.

Monroe watched Leon test the air, and Leon shook his head—

though Monroe hadn't said anything—then stood, looking down the dike to his right. He started along it, and after a few paces, waded into the paddy and hurriedly closed the distance between himself and the treeline.

After a few meters the nipa palm thinned out and Leon stared through the gaps in the trees before him. The place had the feel of an overgrown city park. The canopy kept the undergrowth to a minimum, and several well worn trails ran throughout. Leon waited until everyone was through the nipa palm. A few meters to his left one of the paths curved off toward the open paddies. Through the sparse undergrowth he made out two shallow, mounded bunkers beside the trail. Each bunker was camouflaged with withered palm fronds. The roof of the farthest one had caved in, and both appeared to be unused for a long time. Leon allowed himself to relax a bit.

The smell of damp vegetation was strong: a pungent, heavy odor Leon always found satisfying. He thought it similar to the way summer corn smelled when he and Tucker were kids, moving down the rows of dew-laden tall stalks de-tasseling it as they went. Two bucks an acre and the chance to eat lunches in Axel McCauley's wife's kitchen. Leon and Tucker would come in from the field to platters of fresh chicken, heaps of butter-brown potatoes, thick ears of corn on the cob, peas and baby onions with white sauce, homemade bread topped with sweet strawberry jam, pitchers of ice cold milk, and cherry, apple, or Leon's favorite, lemon pie for dessert.

Thinking about it just then damn near brought Leon to tears. He was hungrier than he'd ever been in his life, and suddenly sick to death of living with the fear that at any moment something horrible might be about to happen.

"Screw it, Monroe," Leon said in disgust. "Let's get our butts home."

With that he started off in a quick but cautious pace for the open paddies.

From his perch high in a tree, Sau Ban watched the squad emerge from the other side of the treeline and file off through the paddies. When he'd seen the American soldiers coming to the place where he'd spent the night—after sending the rest of his men back to the Dinh Ba Forest to await his return—he'd quickly climbed the tree. Experience had taught him it was the safest place to hide.

He knew when the soldiers moved through they were too busy watching for booby-traps on the ground to ever think of looking up. And the squad had passed so close beneath him that he could have spit on their helmets. While he watched them leave, he smiled at his cleverness. He had a good idea they were all going to the same place. The soldiers weren't the only ones heading for Tan Tru. Sau Ban had business in the vicinity as well. He only wished he had the soldier's freedom to travel openly across the paddies. They would most likely reach Tan Tru before noon; restricted to using the treelines, Sau Ban wouldn't arrive until after dark. No matter. Tay Ninh couldn't receive him till then anyway. There was little need to hurry.

Chapter 7

The officer's hootch occupied a spot on the outer edge of Charlie Company's area. There on its front steps rested Lieutenant Stanley Clayborn, 1st platoon's leader.

He was bare-chested, and his fatigues were rolled to mid-calf. He wore an ill-fitting boonie hat, and his gray-framed army issue glasses were propped on his forehead. His Adam's apple protruded from his neck, shuttling up and down beneath a pointy chin, while he stared down at his battered feet. Flakes of pinkish-white skin peeled from his toes like the outer layers of an onion. In his left hand he held an olive-drab tube of ointment. Clayborn rubbed the cream gently between his toes. The medication made them sting, and he rested his heels on the bottom step, waving his feet back and forth until they were dry.

Clayborn was a few years older than the men under his command. He was twenty-four, and at one time he'd planned on making the Army his career. Back in the states, he'd been passed over for promotion once, and Clayborn understood this meant his future in the military was all but finished. Leadership capabilities questionable, one evaluation said. Lacks motivation and the desire for excellence, said another. His wife Sheila encouraged, then pleaded with him to volunteer for Vietnam, knowing full well what it meant. Five months into his tour, Clayborn knew he was not a leader. His men had little respect for him. Leadership was a talent, a gift, like being able to draw, or play an instrument well. It wasn't something to be learned in a classroom, or on a parade field. Leaders were born. Men like Sergeant Drieser had it. The platoon would follow Drieser down the barrel of an artillery piece if they had to, while Clayborn knew they wouldn't follow him to the mess hall. The men blamed him for insisting on sending Connie Doolin and the others up the canal that black night. The men acted withdrawn around him after that, and he couldn't blame them. He hated himself more than they did. For the last few days he'd been composing a letter in his mind, how to word it, a letter to tell Sheila of his decision to resign his commission when his tour was completed.

Clayborn lay back and stretched out in the doorway, hoping the ointment might glue his skin back in place, at least for a little while. He closed his eyes and thought about Sheila, how to break the news. These days, whenever he thought about her, she always appeared stark naked behind his eyes. This surprised and pleased him. He'd never before thought of her in such a purely physical sense. But there she was, in all her naked inviting beauty, the weight of her thighs surrounding his hips, her damp scent on clean sheets, long brown hair splayed over his face. His hand rubbed at the crotch of his fatigues while he tried to think of a safe place where he might go to relieve the pressure. Masturbating was something he'd been doing a lot of recently, more from boredom than anything.

Suddenly, Clayborn knew—no, could feel himself being watched. When he jerked to a sitting position, the heavy glasses dropped painfully to the bridge of his nose, and he nearly knocked heads with Tucker, who hovered over him, a wad of gum in one cheek, and a crooked grin on the other.

What next? Clayborn said to himself. On top of everything else the men thought of him, now this, caught playing with himself like Bastard. The idea made him shrink away from Tucker's gaze.

Clayborn folded his arms clumsily over his lap and assumed a look of innocence.

"Burdick." Clayborn said, attempting to mask the embarrassment in his voice. His foot came to rest on one knee, the erection pressing uncomfortably against the inside of his thigh.

Tucker said nothing, only stared at Clayborn's sore foot. The breakfast of powdered scrambled eggs and bacon fried as hard as a tongue depressor were already launching gas bubbles into Tucker's clogged system, but at least Boyle was out of sight for the time being.

"Well, what is it?" Clayborn said, angrily recovering his composure.

Tucker raised one unlaced boot to the step and stared down at Clayborn's sore foot. He jabbed a finger in the middle of the sole, and Clayborn winced.

"Got yourself some feet there, Lieutenant," Tucker said, blowing a pink bubble that snapped loudly when he sucked it back into his mouth.

Clayborn's hand went to his foot, rubbing the spot tenderly. At least his erection had faded.

"When's the squad coming in?" Tucker asked, his face so close Clayborn could smell the stale mixture of bubble gum and cigarettes.

"I haven't heard," Clayborn answered, and reached for the tube of ointment. Despite their differences in rank and age, Clayborn always felt inferior whenever he dealt with Tucker, and try as he might, he could never seem to get over the feeling.

"Top says for me to burn the shit tubs this morning, Lieutenant."

"Fine, Burdick, that's a good idea. Get the latrine squared away."

"Or should I wait? Maybe they don't need to be burned right yet? Whatcha think?"

Clayborn threw the ointment tube down. Paste oozed from its nozzle, leaving a small drop on the wood step. "Damn it, Burdick. I don't give a rat's ass one way or the other."

"There it is," Tucker said, his grin softening to a smirk. He reached next to Clayborn and swiped a finger through the ointment, studying it. "Sorta looks like sperm, don't it?"

"I wouldn't know."

"Could be that's what this stuff is? Sposed to be good for the skin, at least that's what a whore told me on R&R a few days back. What the hell was her name, anyway?"

For a moment, the image of Sheila returned and Clayborn forced it away just as quickly.

"I hardly think the military is bottling sperm, Burdick."

"Never know. There's some mighty weird shit goes on around here," Tucker said. "Top tried ordering me to discipline Bastard this morning."

For some time Clayborn suspected the place was turning everyone's brains to mush, his included, though he'd long guessed Boyle might have had mental problems to begin with.

"What'd he want you to do, drop Bastard for push-ups?"

Tucker leaned back, and rolled the ointment between his thumb and forefinger.

"I don't think Bastard knows how to do push-ups, Lieutenant," he said, and sniffed his fingers so delicately Clayborn laughed.

"I was making a joke."

Tucker wiped his fingers across his chest. "Well, I'll be burning shit if you need me for anything."

Clayborn waited until Tucker had put some distance between them before slipping on a clean sock. When he looked for the second one, it was missing. He stood up painfully on one foot, glancing over the floor behind him. In a moment, he turned and stared after Burdick.

It had been Burdick who'd found Connie Doolin's arm the morning after the ambush on the canal. Burdick who carried the thing—blown off just below the shoulder by a burst of AK fire—to where Clayborn sat hunched over a map. Burdick who dropped the arm in front of him, the sound of it a dull slap when it landed. At times, Clayborn still heard that sound: and figured he always would. The high-school class ring on the finger, blood splattered over the arm like obscene freckles. Burdick turned and walked away that morning on the canal: walked away as if what he'd just done was the most ordinary thing in the world.

Tucker whistled a happy tune of his own design, and set to work quickly, raising the three trap doors at the back of the latrine which provided access to the waste tubs. He used a steel rod to hook and slide the tubs from beneath the place, then poured diesel fuel into each from a five-gallon Jerry can. Once the fuel had soaked well enough into the mess, Tucker fired them up with a stick match, and stepped back, waiting as the flames grew, the putrid black smoke rising high above the latrine. With a quick glance over his shoulder to see if anyone might be watching, he pulled Clayborn's sock from his pants pocket, and tossed it in the first burning tub.

Chapter 8

Shortly before noon, Boyle stepped from the CQ shack. The sun had opened the sky, increasing the ever-present heat and humidity which always caused him to sweat like a steel worker.

Tucker wasn't the only one to receive a letter he didn't want to read. Boyle had one, too. A missive from Gloria, a letter detailing the list of things she intended to take in the divorce. From the looks of it, she wanted damn near everything Boyle had, even his imported Bavarian walnut cribbage board, the very board Boyle purchased when he was fourteen, using the money he'd won out-cheating his father once he'd caught on to the old geezer's game. The letter depressed him, and he needed something to make him feel better, and since it was too soon in the day to get drunk, he went outside to clear his thoughts.

The steps of the CQ afforded Boyle a vantage point from which he could scan the entire company area, and he did, looking here and there at the ramshackle hootches, the five-hundred-gallon tank of the company's shower. On top of a bunker, two men sat, one cleaned his rifle, the other was writing a letter, the paper spread awkwardly on his knee. Finally Boyle's gaze fell on the laundry hootch. Maybe it was time to pay another visit to Tay Ninh? He hooked both thumbs over his web gun-belt and took a pose like a town marshall. For Boyle, sex ran a dead heat with good whiskey, and since good whiskey happened to be in short supply, Tay Ninh might be just the thing to make him forget his problems.

Boyle hurried down the path leading to the NCO hootch. Once inside, he quickly changed into his cleanest set of dirty fatigues, threw open his footlocker and splashed on the Old Spice after-shave Gloria had sent for his thirty-ninth birthday: though exactly why she thought he might care how he smelled in this place, he'd never appreciated until now.

On his way to the laundry he spotted Douh, 1st platoon's Vietnamese Tiger Scout, napping in the shade of bunker 10.

At the moment, Douh was dreaming of a train ride he'd taken as a young boy, his father pointing out the window while Douh sat sucking on a peppermint stick. When Douh cracked an eyelid, he half expected to see his father standing there instead of Boyle.

"On your feet, Doe-doe," Boyle frowned at him. "This ain't the church picnic. Stand-to!"

The dream seemed real enough that, awake or not, Douh thought he could still smell the coal fire of the steam engine. He soon decided the fiery smell was from the dark cloud of diesel smoke drifting over the camp where Delta company was burning their tubs for the day.

"What is happening, Top?" Douh said, mimicking how the soldiers greeted each other, unaware Boyle hated to be spoken to that way.

"What's happening is this, Doe-doe. I'm on my way to see Tay Ninh, and you're going to do the talking."

Boyle continually pronounced Douh's name the way it had accidentally been spelled on the documents Douh had carried with him to Tan Tru. He'd long since given up on getting Boyle to soften the O sound and say it right.

"It is *dow*, First Sergeant," he'd said, correcting him the first day they had met. They were in the CQ at the time. Boyle seemed a little put out at first that Douh could speak English so well, and the conversation that day had quickly degenerated, like most conversations with Boyle, into something else.

"Dow," Douh said again, pleasantly. "Like the people who make your napalm. Dow Chemical."

"Dow, huh? Sure as hell ain't spelled that way," Boyle said, scowling at the forms Douh had handed him.

"Because it is Vietnamese, First Sergeant," Douh answered, not knowing about the typo.

"I'll give you that," Boyle said. "But you're with an American unit now, and we pronounce things the way they're spelled. You want people to say your name right around here, then you oughta spell it right. Don't you think?"

"I do spell it right."

"Well it ain't natural. See if I was standing in my kitchen back home and my wife was making bread, how do you think it would sound if I said: 'Gee, Honey, what are you gonna do with all that bread dow?' "

"That would be wrong, First Sergeant."

"My point, exactly. D-o-u-g-h is dough. It's not my fault your parents spelled your name wrong."

With Douh following reluctantly behind, Boyle headed on for Tay Ninh's. Douh knew Boyle wasn't going to collect his laundry, because he never turned any in.

On Wednesdays, after taking his shower for the week, Boyle would strap the .45 below his belly like a truss, and walk naked to see his buddy Shoals in the supply shack located a few meters behind the laundry. Since Shoals was three figures in debt to Boyle and his cribbage board, he was always ready with a new set of fatigues when Boyle came calling. The used ones Shoals passed out to anyone who wanted them: though no one else was round enough to wear them.

Shower day had become something of an event for the three mamasans who policed trash in Charlie's company area, because Boyle would invariably find an excuse to parade past them, each time sending the three old women into a tittering, huddle of ducks at the spectacle.

Boyle did make for a comical sight. He would throw out his chest, set his legs apart like his groin was suddenly chafed, and strut by, convinced he was still a fine figure of the man he thought himself to be.

Tay Ninh's laundry was a scaled-down version of the platoon hootches. A twelve-inch plank served as a counter spanning a wall constructed from flattened beer cans, which were interlocked to form a colorful tin quilt. On the floor, stacked in neat rows, were bundles of faded green fatigues, folded and tied with strips of palm frond.

No one knew where Tay Ninh did all this laundry. She'd never been seen washing any of it. Somehow, on laundry day, the fatigues she took in during the week were back, all neatly folded, and all with a new sourness about them.

Inside the laundry, Boyle got right to the point. "Go on. Ask her, Doe-doe" he said, shaking back his shoulders.

Tay Ninh looked up from the counter and the laundry list she pretended to study, nodded politely at Boyle, then Douh, who stared at his feet.

Tall for a Vietnamese, Tay Ninh stood eye to eye with Boyle, and could maybe even look down on him a little. She was in her mid twenties. Blue-black hair touched her waist. Her eyes were large and almond-shaped beneath long lashes, and they were the color of good coffee. She carried herself with a dreamy aloofness, a quality Boyle found irresistible. Unfortunately for him, Tay Ninh considered Boyle very resistible, and so far had turned down every sum of money he'd offered her.

Tay Ninh spoke as much English as she needed to, and of course she already knew what Boyle was doing there. She also knew Douh became tongue-tied whenever he was around her. Each time he came to collect his laundry he stammered his way through the transaction, too shy even to look at her.

"Come on," Boyle said. "I ain't got all day. Ask her."

Douh cleared his throat and spoke to her in Vietnamese. "*Tay Ninh, the first sergeant has a wish.*" As usual, he couldn't meet her gaze.

"*Oh? Does he wish for me to do his laundry?*" she said, and grinned at his obvious discomfort.

"*No.*"

Tay Ninh flashed a smile at Boyle, which he assumed meant the negotiations were going well.

"What's she saying?"

"I am searching for the right words, Top."

"Words? Here's all the words she needs." Boyle pulled a roll of military payment certificate from his pocket and thumbed it. "Fifty bucks, Doe-doe. Not a penny more. Tell her that."

Tay Ninh nodded at the money. "*Now, I see,*" she said, turning to Douh. "*He wishes to BUY my laundry.*"

Douh knew she was toying with him and it made him angry enough to speak plainly. "*Please, I am embarrassed enough. You know what the first sergeant has come for.*"

"*And what have you come for, Douh? Are you here to watch?*"

"*No. Of course not.*"

"*Then what are you doing with this water buffalo?*"

"*I am the interpreter.*"

Tay Ninh laughed.

Boyle grinned like an idiot.

"*A fine interpreter,*" she said. "*You have difficulty asking for your laundry.*"

Douh looked back to his feet, and Boyle leaned closer, leering at Tay Ninh.

"Is she going for it?"

"She is thinking about it, Top."

"Well, tell her not to think too long. I got work to do."

Douh turned back to Tay Ninh. This time he looked into her face.

"*I do not want to be here. Please tell me something so I can go away.*"

"*Very well,*" she said, the smile dropping from her lips. "*Tell him there is not enough money in his country for me to do what he wants. And tell him his little bird is so small that I would not feel it if I did.*"

"*I cannot tell him that!*"

"*No? Then YOU do what he wants,*" she said, and in a swirl of hair, stepped into a back room office and out of sight.

Boyle peeled money from his roll. "Fifty it is."

"Yes . . . fifty," Douh said, stalling for time. "But there is a problem."

"She want more?" Boyle said.

"She thinks you are very generous."

Boyle stopped apprehensively in mid-count. "What is it, then?"

"The problem is with Tay Ninh."

"Damn it, Doe-doe, what the hell are you talking about? She was giving me the come on," Boyle snapped.

"Yes, Top. Tay Ninh says she finds you desirable."

"I knew it! So what's wrong?"

"The problem is with Tay Ninh. She—" Suddenly an idea popped into Douh's head that he hoped would be a solution to his predicament.

Rumors of some sort continually circulated among the men of the company. Some were true, while others, like most rumors, were not. One that was not true, but all the men chose to believe anyway, was about an incurable form of something called Black Syphilis. According to the latest version, men who caught it were sent to an island—the name of which, of course, no one seemed to know—

somewhere in the middle of the Pacific. There they lived in agony, while penises rotted like over-ripe bananas. The rumor also had it the Viet Cong infected prostitutes with the disease as part of their war effort, though many of the men figured—or at least hoped— this last part to be untrue.

"She is not well. Tay Ninh is very sick," Douh said quickly.

"Looked healthy enough to me," Boyle mumbled, peeking behind the counter to see where she had gone. "What's she doing, anyway?"

"Tay Ninh is too ashamed to be here when I tell you."

It began to dawn on Boyle that another of his plans was about to go awry. "All right, Doe-doe! Spit it out!"

"Yes. Tay Ninh says to tell you that she regrets that she has a disease."

Boyle pondered the word for a good while as if the thought hadn't occurred to him before. Slowly his face assumed a frightened look, and he motioned at his crotch.

"You mean. . .with her snatch?"

Douh looked to where Boyle pointed. "Yes. Her. . .her snatch, it is not well."

Boyle ran a hand over his mouth, peeked into the back room, and a growing look of dread crossed his face.

"Is it—"

"Yes. The worst kind," Douh said.

Boyle shook the last Lucky from the pack in his breast pocket and stared with a thoughtful expression into Tay Ninh's small empty office. This always seemed to be the way these things went for him. Nothing in life ever worked out the way he would have liked it to. His list of failures seemed longer than most anyone else's he could think of, and he could never quite place his finger on the reason why.

Before he had time to reach for his lighter, Douh had his own Zippo out, waving flame over the end of the cigarette for him.

"Damn," Boyle said, after a long drag. "And to think—" The thought was too horrible for him to consider. He blew smoke across the room and moved quickly for the door. To hell with the time of day, he was going to get drunk, well, tipsy at least.

Outside, the sun had reached its highest point in the sky, but the air felt cooler than under the canvas roof of the laundry. Boyle stared through Douh for a moment, and the pained expression on his face gradually softened to one of relief.

"By God, I owe you one there, Doe-doe."

Douh grinned and nodded. He'd found a way to save face, while at the same time shaking Boyle off Tay Ninh's scent once and for all.

"Sure she ain't just got a dose of the clap or something?" Boyle asked, as if that wouldn't be so bad.

Douh stared down at the path and shook his head.

"Damn," Boyle said once more. "Wouldn't ya know it. Just when she was coming around."

"Am I dismissed now, Top?" Douh said.

"Yeah . . . yeah, sure," Boyle said.

But before Douh could take his leave, Boyle suddenly grabbed his arm, eyes narrowed in suspicion. "You and her ain't fucking with me now, are you?"

Douh shook his head earnestly. "Tay Ninh would never make jokes about something like this, Top."

Boyle ran his gaze over the area for a few moments. "Yeah. I suppose not. Ah, what the hell," he said, tugging his gun belt back under his stomach. "Stand 'em on their heads and they all look like sisters. Right, Doe-doe?" He slapped Douh on the back hard enough to make him stagger.

"Yes, Top. That is true," Douh said, and forced a grin.

They walked to where the path branched toward the NCO hootch and Boyle took it.

"Stop by my quarters tonight, Doe-doe, and I'll buy you a drink," he yelled over his shoulder.

"We shall drink to your good health, First Sergeant," Douh called back, and he waited until Boyle disappeared inside the hootch.

Chapter 9

Douh was a Chieu Hoi. With the help of the American mission in Saigon, a program had been developed whereby enemy soldiers could be repatriated into the Republic. It was called Open Arms, or Chieu Hoi. As a young student, Douh studied English in Hanoi, hoping someday he might realize his dream of attending Stanford University in the States. His dream was to become a poet. But any chance of that ended when the first American marines landed in 1965 and the war began in earnest.

In 1967 Douh soon found himself drafted into the North Vietnamese Army. After two months training he'd been sent south on the Ho Chi Minh Trail with a hundred other soldiers. The trip lasted three months: traveling mostly at night to dodge air strikes and ambushes. By the time they arrived on the Cambodian border and were ready to cross into the Mekong Delta, malaria and dysentery had killed along the way what the U.S. and ARVN soldiers hadn't. There were only twenty-five of them now, and they broke into five-man teams, again, traveling at night, this time using sanpans to navigate a myriad of streams and canals while making their way toward Saigon.

For seven nights they moved through the Plain of Reeds. Douh had never been this far south before and he hated the water that seemed to be everywhere he looked or stepped. The land here was so low that rivers and canals rose and fell with the tide. The stench of delta mud clung to him with a closeness he found nearly overpowering. He missed the mountains and clear streams of the North so much that sometimes he'd wander off to sit alone, composing sentimental poems about home that always made him sad enough to cry.

On the northern edge of the Plain of Reeds, in the village of Ap Vinh Ho, Douh and his companions met up with the local Viet Cong who took them into Saigon where they set them up with forged identification papers and a safe-house. Their hideout was located just off the traffic circle formed by the juncture of Tran Hung Dao Street and Le Loi, on the edge of the Chinese Cholon district of the city.

Because of his command of English, Douh prowled the city alone, learning to navigate its streets and alleyways, while his compatriots worked in the safe-house, building bombs.

In the evenings, before curfew, he'd return, relating what he'd seen. He mapped out the names and locations of places where groups of American soldiers congregated.

Douh never tired of roving through the city. He loved the freedom he had during the day. Saigon was a place of endless fascination for him. Everywhere the streets were filled with sounds and smells. The air hung thick with the exhaust fumes of the vehicles that swarmed everywhere: Renault taxis, jeeps, military trucks, Honda motorcycles. It sounded as if everyone drove with one hand pressing the horn while jockeying for position in the thick traffic.

Many of the motorcyclists wore narrow-toed, block-heeled shoes, tight pants, and long-sleeved white shirts with the cuffs tucked under in the style of the Saigon Cowboy. They kept a ready supply of American cigarettes dangling from the corners of their lips, and dark wrap-around Ray Ban sunglasses on their eyes.

Now and then a rider would zip by toting a young woman side-saddle on the seat behind him, her conical straw hat held firmly with one hand, while the hem of her white *ao dai* fluttered flag-like beside the bikes rear wheel. At those moments Douh wished to feel what the driver felt. The girl pressed into his back, her breasts touching him there, just beneath the shoulder blades.

If he walked past the bars on Tu Do Street, the voices of B-girls promising American soldiers beaucoup boom-boom for ti-ti money never failed to arouse him. It had been a long time since he'd spent time with a woman, and each day it was becoming more difficult to force the ache from his mind.

The odors that sifted from the bars as he strolled along the street came at him like a thick brown wind. He could smell the cheap perfume the whores covered themselves with, and the ripe smell of the soldiers' cigarettes and sweat. He saw how the B-girls shaded their eyes with makeup to appear less oriental for the Americans. A number of bars had bands playing in them. The Vietnamese musicians did their best to imitate American rock and roll. They strummed electric guitars while forming their mouths awkwardly around foreign syllables, sounding as if they were doing a parody of themselves. On raised platforms over the bar, girls with hair piled in rows of curls danced in mini-skirts and halter tops which raised their small breasts to ridiculous angles. Juke boxes blasted music from doorways to mix with the sounds of the street until there wasn't anything but sound, sound that seemed as necessary to this setting as the sun above, and the tamarind trees that looked so out of place growing from the curbs.

Here and there, young boys walked with balloon-covered sticks, and screamed English obscenities any time a passing soldier popped a balloon with a cigarette. Children of all ages milled about: some eating pink cotton candy, others slurping in a race against the heat on banana Popsicles.

Douh sometimes tucked himself into a doorway where he could watch the street hustlers working the throngs of soldiers. Everything had a price. One day a boy, who looked to be no older than nine, approached Douh and offered a sixty-millimeter mortar for twenty American dollars. When Douh said he had no use for such things, the boy offered his sister—who he promised was a number one cherry-girl—for half the price.

On the curbs, vendors squatted in front of small displays holding cartons of Salem cigarettes, Canadian Club whiskey, Ivory detergent, and bars of Palmolive bath soap. Old men pedaled pedicabs through the streets, while the soldiers they carried in front of them held PX-purchased Nikon cameras to their faces: snapping pictures for the folks back home.

One day, when Douh happened to be making his way back across town to the safe-house, three Air Force privates accosted him. They were drunk, and spoke to him in pidgin English, explaining how they were going back to the world and wanted a picture together. Though they slapped each other on the back jovially, and swore they would always stay in touch, Douh knew what they knew. The soldiers would never see each other again, and the photo might someday be all they had to prove they'd ever been there at all.

Douh posed between them, grinning stupidly and flashing the peace sign while the pedicab driver took their picture.

Day after day Douh watched this carnival-like atmosphere, and each day he began to feel more a part of it. No one paid him any mind while he wandered throughout the city. He found if he kept moving, then he could travel anywhere without so much as a glance from any of the hundreds of MP's, or the White Mice of Saigon's police force asking to see his papers.

By the end of the third week of his wanderings, Douh made up his mind to defect. He'd never wanted to be a soldier. Absolutely nothing about it satisfied him. To his way of thinking the entire country was Vietnam. North. South. What did it matter? And Douh figured he faced a better chance of someday making it to Stanford if he stayed where he was, so his decision was made. He'd Chieu Hoi the first chance he got.

That same night he failed to return to the safe-house, and instead, hid in an alley off Tu Do Street. It happened to be Douh's misfortune to have picked an alley beneath the open windows of a whorehouse. The narrow passageway echoed with the sounds of drunken copulations till long into the night, causing him to spend a large portion of it in a state of arousal. Not that he might have slept anyway: not with all the rats sharing the alley with him. Hundreds of them rattled everywhere through the stacks of garbage.

At last morning arrived with Douh watching from the alley's entrance for the first American soldier to come by. He didn't have long to wait. Around 0630 two soldiers strode down the street toward Douh's hiding place. Their fatigues were coated in a permanent layer of red dust; their jungle boots, worn clean of shine, were caked with peanut-butter-colored mud. They each carried M-16's, but Douh noticed, with some relief, that they didn't have clips in them.

Douh moved from his hiding place just as the soldiers turned for the whorehouse door. He held the Chieu Hoi poster torn from a wall earlier, and saying the first five words of English that came into his mouth—"Take me. I am yours"—he emerged cautiously from the alley. Douh realized immediately, given the circumstances, those words probably weren't his best choice for an opening statement, but the sight of the soldiers made him so nervous he forgot the speech he'd passed a good portion of the night rehearsing. At any rate, the soldiers seemed not to notice. They were a little put out, however, at taking a prisoner so early in the morning.

After some debate about what to do with him, the soldiers decided on dropping Douh off at the first MP station they came across, and a pedicab driver dousing in his cab down the street was hailed into service. As defections went, Douh expected a bit more drama than having the three of them ride along a nearly deserted Tu Do Street, Douh sitting between his two cheerless captors, while he, the soldiers, and the pedicab driver all smoked his cigarettes.

As it turned out, the Americans had less need for a poet than their counterparts to the north. Douh spent another six months at a repatriation camp outside of Long Binh before being assigned to the 9th Division as an interpreter and scout.

Now the duck fat was really in the fire. Douh prayed for the South's victory. If not, he had little doubt as to what his former comrades would do if they ever got their hands on him. All but one had been arrested after Douh led the MP's to the safe-house, and he knew it was foolish to think any of them would ever lay eyes on each other again, but still, Douh was disturbed by the fact that one escaped capture by leaving for the delta a day before. And that's what troubled him. He and Sau Ban were in the same part of the country once again. Douh didn't like any of it.

Chapter 10

A little past midday Leon led the squad out of the treeline far to the west of Tan Tru and into the final leg of their march. Tucker spotted them when they were a good distance away, but he knew Leon had the point. That loose, loping gate of his was easy to pick out. Tucker allowed himself to relax a bit seeing his friend. Things were getting back to normal.

Bastard also had a view of the squad coming in. He sat perched on the end peek of 1st platoon's roof, busy licking his wounds. Earlier he'd wandered into the cool darkness of a bunker to escape the afternoon heat. He'd been attacked immediately by three rats who bit his toes and tail without mercy until he'd been driven off.

Leaning back on the roof, Bastard lifted a foot to his mouth and licked a blood-caked toe. The men were close enough for him to hear their voices. He paid them little mind.

Tucker had finished telling what was worth telling about his R&R, and he, Leon, and Monroe were sharing a warm beer on Leon's cot while they brought Tucker up to speed on what had happened the week he'd been gone. Nothing. So much nothing that even Leon admitted a little contact with the enemy would be a welcome break to the endless monotony.

Conroy was wearing a pair of olive-drab boxers, and singing. "Witchita Lineman" played from the radio on his lap while his head swayed expressively with the song.

"Look at the man," Monroe said, holding the beer out for anyone who wanted it. "Sitting down there singing along with that sad-ass shit. You watch. He gonna be crying by the time he's through."

Leon agreed the song was sad. And it seemed any time the radio played these days, "Wichita Lineman" was on. The last thing he needed to hear was a song about being lonely. He'd written his former girlfriend Lorie at least twice a month since he'd been in-country, thinking the least she could do, given the circumstances, would be to answer. She never did.

Like Monroe had predicted, when the song ended and Conroy glanced back at them, his eyes were puffy.

"You gonna make yourself sick listening to that shit, Conroy," Monroe called to him.

"I love that song," Conroy called back in a squeaky voice.

"That ain't no lie. You blubbering away like some pink-face little baby every time it come on."

Monroe shook his head. "I'm telling you, the man is without soul." Monroe looked for the beer just as Leon finished it, belching loudly once the can left his lips. Monroe stared at Conroy's back with a look of remorse both Tucker and Leon noticed.

"You ever hear Conroy talk about his girlfriend?" Monroe said.

Leon looked up at Conroy, who lay staring at the ceiling.

"No," Leon said.

"He got one, you know," Monroe said, continuing to eye Conroy.

"So?" Tucker said.

Monroe's face scrunched up a little. "Damn, Tucker. How can you see a man as homely as Conroy an' not wonder what the girl look like that gonna think he look good? How the hell he gonna kiss her with them teeth a his?"

Tucker had to admit Monroe did have a point. He peeked over his shoulder in Conroy's direction.

"My mom always said there's someone for everyone. And if you don't believe me. . .just look around," Leon said.

"I hear ya, brother." Monroe chuckled, and ran his palm over his scalp, checking for stubble. "There's some ugly motherfuckers in this world."

Monroe bent over and unlaced his boot. "One time back on the block there was this girl. Clarissa Gates." He tugged the boot from his foot with a grunt, and stared through the front of the hootch.

"Sweet Clarissa. Man, I started sweating in places a man ain't supposed to sweat every time I was in the same room with the girl." He brought his other boot up to rest on his knee and worked on its laces.

"One time I got myself looking good, an' I go on over to her crib. Her father come to the screen door when I knock."

He tossed the second boot near the first, and he rubbed his foot. "I never took her out before, but he knows me from the neighborhood. We stand there looking each other over for a bit, an' I'm thinking that Clarissa musta been adopted or something, cause this is the ugliest man I ever seen. He says to me, What you want, Monroe? I says, I come to take Clarissa out on a date. Then you know what he did?" Monroe dropped his foot to the floor, not waiting for an answer.

"The man is holding a can of this bug spray shit and he says, Go away, Monroe, then he sprays me through the screen with the stuff." Monroe leaned forward and rested his elbows on his knees and stared at his feet.

"You take her out after that?" Leon asked.

"What kind of a fool you take me for?" Monroe grumbled, lying back on the cot. "How am I going back over there after what that man did to me?" He scratched beneath his chin, thoughtfully. "Whole thing was humiliating."

Monroe pulled his feet onto the cot and folded his hands behind his head.

"Burdick!" Boyle shouted from the doorway just then.

Tucker muttered something under his breath before twisting around to face him. "What is it, Top?"

"Thought I told you to police the bunkers?"

"You told me to burn the shit tubs."

Tucker thought quickly for a moment, then added: "Let somebody else do the bunkers." He slid back around, and waited for Boyle to rise to the bait, knowing he wouldn't take any back talk if there were an audience.

"Sooo, that's it, is it?" Boyle said, and closed the distance between them in a hurry.

"Think you're running the company, do you? Well, Burdick, that mouth of yours just talked you into OP duty tomorrow," Boyle sneered, glancing from one to the other with an angry, satisfied look. His eyes settled on Leon, and then to Monroe. Both wore silly, innocent expressions, hoping they were next, and Boyle didn't disappoint them.

"What are you two grinning about? You can keep him company."

While Boyle paused for their whining to stop, he ran his eyes over the place, and took his time about it. "Conroy!" Boyle yelled over his shoulder.

Conroy raised his head from the cot, half asleep. "Yeah, Top?"

"I want you to get this area squared away tomorrow."

Monroe jerked to a sitting position as if he'd been poked in the back. "Tomorrow!"

"That's right," Boyle said, peeking at all three of them with a sly grin. "Clayborn volunteered the squad for the boats. Night insertion. First platoon has the bunker guard, and 2nd squad is off until eighteen-hundred tomorrow."

Boyle let out an evil-sounding laugh. "That's right, smart guys. And you'll be back in time to catch the boat before it leaves."

With that, Boyle did an about-face and stormed out, stumbling over, then kicking an empty C-ration carton on the way.

"Asshole," Monroe said, and rested back on his cot once Boyle had cleared the building. "We just done fucked up a day off."

Leon glared at Tucker's sheepish expression with disgust. "Damn it all, anyway," he said, and launched a cracked helmet liner the length of the hootch and out the door with a swift kick from his bare foot. He then threw himself on his cot with a reckless bounce. Nothing more was said for a time, until for some reason, Monroe sat up suddenly and looked outside.

"What's that fool doing?" Monroe said, and pointed outside.

Tucker eased himself up a bit and looked to where Boyle stood in the latrine, his hands cupped over his eyes, staring down all the holes.

Tucker stretched out on his cot, his poncho liner bunched beneath his head. "He's looking for a fly."

On the other side of Tucker, Leon, despite his anger, snorted his way to the beginnings of a deep snore.

"Tell me something, Monroe," Tucker said quietly, up on one elbow, and staring out the opposite torn screen. "Why do you suppose Clayborn volunteers the platoon for every shitty job that comes down the pike?"

Monroe considered the question for a moment or two. "Guilt," he said finally.

"Guilt?"

"Sure," Monroe said.

"What's guilt got to do with it?"

"Got everything to do with it. You know how they say the criminal always returns to the scene of the crime?"

"Yeah."

"Ask me, Clayborn's sort of doing the same thing." Monroe poked a Salem in his mouth and lit it. A bluish smoke ring floated above, and Monroe launched a smaller ring through it like a bull's-eye. "The man thinks he fucked up the night Doolin got shot."

"You think he didn't?"

"No," Monroe said, his lips formed around the word. "And Clayborn don't neither. That's what keeps him wanting to go back out there. You know he extended to stay on the line for another six months?"

"He was due to rotate!" Tucker said.

Monroe rolled over and ground the cigarette out on the floor. "Guilt, my man. He'd stay here forever if they let him, and he don't even know it." Monroe leaned back on an elbow, taking the same position as Tucker. "We all going to live with it, Tucker. Maybe not at first, but as time goes on I guess we're all going to have a measure of it."

Tucker kicked back once more, and tried to think if there were anything he felt guilty enough about that would make him extend his tour. He came up empty and chased the thought away.

"I think we ought to party tonight," Monroe said to change the subject. "Conroy's got a case of beer in his footlocker, and I got a half bottle of whiskey in mine. Don't know about you and Leon, but me an' Conroy are fixing to get ourselves drunk. Get Higgins to bring the tunes. He's always ready for a good time." Monroe rolled over with his back to Tucker. "I need to grab some Z's, my man. If you see Preach, tell him I want that bean."

And just that quickly, he fell to sleep.

Down the way, Conroy's radio played over the sound of Leon's snoring. Overhead a chopper thumped across the camp, hammering on into the distance for a good while until its sound was steadily taken over by the camp generator. In the meanwhile, Tucker gazed at the ceiling until he realized what he was looking at. The profile of Bastard was shadowed there on the sunlit canvas above.

Monkeys—flies—beans—guilt. None of it made sense and Tucker didn't feel sleepy anymore. He eased himself between the cots and went outside to feed Pearl's monkey.

Chapter 11

A humid wind rattled the trees and nipa palm along the Song Vam Co Tay, and as it did, Sau Ban searched for the tunnel entrance hidden in the darkness of the river's north bank. He would find it. A month had passed since the night he'd managed the task with nothing more to go on other than Tay Ninh's instructions that the entrance lay twenty paces to the right of the path running down from the base camp. But this time low clouds reflected what light there was from the camp, and in a matter of minutes Sau Ban found the entrance. He drew back the cover—palm fronds woven to look like any pile of dead vegetation along the river—and stared down at the round black hole.

The entrance pit dropped nearly three meters, and Sau Ban braced his body with hands and feet on either side of its walls, lowering himself until he touched the tunnel floor.

At first, the urge to flee the claustrophobic space was strong, but after a few deep breaths to calm his fear, Sau Ban felt for the tunnel to his left, forced himself to all fours, and set off at a crawl.

The tunnel was old, though still in fairly stable condition. The air was rank with damp rot. The farther he crawled, the tighter the air felt entering his lungs. Tay Ninh's father—a province chief and member of the Viet Minh during the war against the French—had helped dig this very tunnel. But the shaft had been fitted for smaller men than Sau Ban. Sections of the passage pinched his shoulders, and he found it necessary to turn sideways in order to fit through. These were the times when Sau Ban steeled himself to keep going. It was easy to imagine becoming wedged like a cork, and bile kept rising to his throat at the thought.

While he crawled, the hard, coarse soil scraped knees and shins, the walls scratched skin from his shoulders and arms. Dirt sifted from the ceiling and into his eyes and nose. Several times he stopped to sneeze violently, the sound muffled and dead as a grave.

Now and then there were bamboo tubes through the ceiling. He paused below each, breathing a deep lungful of air, nearly giddy at the sweet taste.

Sau Ban had been crawling for nearly a half-hour when the tunnel vibrated. He froze in place, sure the tunnel was caving in until he remembered Tay Ninh saying proudly how the tunnel passed near the American's artillery. The tunnel shuddered around him once more. A chunk of clay fell onto his head, and he hurried on, forgetting the pain in his shoulders and legs for the time being.

Dim light filtered through the cracks of the trap door in Tay Ninh's house. Sau Ban uncurled himself, pressing his ear to the wood planks above. Music was playing, Tay Ninh's signal that all was well. Sau Ban pressed the top of his head against the flooring and stood, opening the trap door a fraction of an inch. Tay Ninh swung in a white nylon hammock on the far side of the rose-colored, stucco-walled room. She rocked herself from side to side with one slender foot dangling to the floor. Her clothes were made of glossy black silk, the blouse collarless, the pants loose and comfortable. Her long hair spilled to the wood floor from the side of the hammock, the tips of it brushing a lazy pattern in the dust. She seemed engrossed with something on the wall. And not until Sau Ban had disengaged himself from the hole, and stood shaking dirt from his shorts did she look at him.

"Oh," she said, examining him with a dreamy gaze. "A groundhog has come to visit."

Sau Ban felt a familiar tension swell like a balloon in his chest. Keep it away, he told himself, and he took several deep breaths before turning to face her.

"I envy your comforts, Tay Ninh," Sau Ban said, dusting his hands.

From the top of an ancient looking four-drawer bureau that normally concealed the tunnel entrance, a hurricane lamp cast the room in amber. Sticks of incense curled smoke from a small table in the corner, the thick smell quickly erasing the foul tunnel air from Sau Ban's nostrils. In one corner, a small sandbag bunker stood. Its square bulk took up a good portion of the room, and appeared out of place, but necessary. On the table beside the incense, a transistor radio played American music. Sau Ban turned the radio off.

Tay Ninh continued to rock as if she were alone. "You do not care for my taste in music, Sau Ban?" Her voice, like her gaze, had a faraway quality about it.

Sau Ban grunted an answer and pulled a high-backed chair from the table, leaning back in it, his feet assuming a casual position on the floor.

From time to time, the sound of men's voices could be heard rising over the din of the camp's generator. The arrogant fools feel secure enough behind their bunkers and razor wire to carry on as if they were on a field trip, he thought.

"The invaders seem to be enjoying themselves this evening, Tay Ninh."

Laughter and catcalls echoed in the near distance.

"Yes," Tay Ninh murmured, and lifted to a sitting position in the hammock, leaning her back against the wall. One leg of her pants bunched at the knee when her feet dangled over the edge. Her toenails were painted a deep red. Sau Ban caught himself staring at them, and Tay Ninh hugged herself as if suddenly cold.

His eyes were what frightened her. They were lifeless, like they never saw what it was they were looking at.

"And what about you, Sau Ban? What is it you enjoy?"

In spite of his irritation with her, the nonchalance of Tay Ninh's question had a soothing affect, and Sau Ban felt suddenly more at ease. In her home, in the very laps of the Americans, he knew he was as safe, possibly safer, as he would be with his men back in the Dinh Ba Forest. His and Tay Ninh's business could wait, there was no rush. He was only human after all, and the company of a beautiful woman wasn't something he found distasteful, even if the woman happened to be the sassy-mouthed Tay Ninh. But she was also an intelligent woman, and Sau Ban relished the opportunity to converse with anyone more worldly than the naive farm boys he was forced to lead.

"In another time, you might be surprised at the things I would enjoy, Tay Ninh," he said, and set his lips in a toothy grin.

Tay Ninh's eyes wandered briefly over the room and closed. Her chin drooped to her chest, like she might be nodding to sleep. With an effort she struggled to raise herself to a more upright position and stretched her neck from side to side before speaking.

"Tell me, Sau Ban. I want to know."

As she said this, the sound of someone singing in the camp

reached them, and Sau Ban stared through the wall in that direction.

"To take this camp away from those overfed bastards. That is one thing I would enjoy," he said in a casual tone.

Tay Ninh laughed a bird-like giggle at this. "And how would you go about it, Sau Ban? Charge with your four-man army?"

Her words stung, and he had to force himself not to respond in kind. She was laughing at him. Sau Ban didn't like it when people laughed at him. He told himself to be calm, and took several more deep breaths before speaking.

"Give me a squad of sappers and a hundred men and I could take it," Sau Ban said defiantly, before adding with a tone of disappointment: "I couldn't hold it, but I could take it just the same."

Tay Ninh cared nothing for what Sau Ban was saying. She already felt smothered by the weight of the war. Everything was war. Each minute of the day was war. Her business and life were driven by it. She had never known a time when there wasn't war. She carried war from the earliest memories of childhood, right up to the last thing she thought of at night. Even her dreams betrayed her, where people died again and again. She hurried to change the direction of the conversation, and began telling Sau Ban something amusing. A story of Boyle and his interpreter's visit that afternoon. She'd been peeking through a hole in the wall at the two of them when Douh told Boyle she had a disease. When she mimicked the first sergeant's expression, even Sau Ban found it humorous, though his face belied the fact. At the moment he happened to be more interested in other things.

"You say the interpreters name is Douh?"

She nodded.

"What do you know about him?"

"Little," Tay Ninh answered. Her eyes closed for a long moment, then she motioned with a loose toss of her arm. "My laundry is in their area. Douh is Charlie Company's scout."

Sau Ban inched forward.

"Describe him for me."

Tay Ninh appeared lost to the question. Her eyes wandered over the room, finally settling on her feet which she raised to the hammock and folded beneath her.

"He has the kind of fat cheeks that mothers enjoy pinching," she said with a vacant smile.

"Does one of his eyebrows have a scar that divides it in half?" Sau Ban asked.

"Yes," Tay Ninh answered. "Do you know him?"

Chapter 12

A forty-watt bulb in the center of 1st platoon's hootch burned dimly. The room held more shadow than light while the men drank at the back of the place. What remained of Monroe's bottle of Old Crow sat in the middle of his footlocker. Beside it, a candle burned from a C-ration can, surrounded by several empty and pinched cans of Falstaff.

Conroy was drunk, and unusually talkative. He'd just finished telling Preacher about how he used to sing a hymn in church that had a line in it about a cross-eyed bear named Gladly. For a few moments the men weren't sure if Conroy was joking or not.

"It's, 'gladly the cross I'd bear,' Conroy," Preacher corrected him before falling into a fit of drunken laughter.

"That ain't funny, then . . . is it?"

Preacher dropped to his knees, performing a silly mime of a bear with his eyes crossed.

Monroe said, "Why would a church song be talking about some cross-eyed bear, man?"

"Well, that's what I always wanted to know," Conroy whined, by now the only one in the room not laughing.

Tucker bummed a smoke from Leon then took a swig of the beer he was nursing. He'd never cared much for drinking. He had a lingering fear of turning into his father, and during those infrequent times when the men were able to let loose, he usually remained sober.

"Conroy, you are one of a kind," Tucker said, grinning at the perplexed expression on Conroy's face.

"Thanks, Tucker," Conroy said, watching Preacher, who by now was over the edge. He lay spread-eagled on the floor, rolling his red face from side to side, laughing so hard he couldn't breathe.

"Hey, Preach," Monroe said after a spell. "Show Tucker that bean, my man."

Preacher rummaged around in his shirt pocket for a moment, finally waving the bean in their direction.

Monroe placed it on the footlocker. "That's the thing, Tucker," he said, then sat back and poured more bourbon into his beer.

Tucker leaned forward, arms on knees, and stared at the vanilla bean.

Just then Higgins drifted through the front door, Douh close behind. Higgins' eyes were bloodshot and puffy behind the lenses of his glasses. In his left hand he carried a battery operated, reel-to-reel tape player.

Douh wore blue shower thongs, and an o.d. green T-shirt that was a few sizes too large. His fatigue pants were rolled to the knees.

Higgins drew up in front of them, while Douh smiled shyly at them all.

"Higgins, my man," Monroe said, eyeing the tape player happily and scooting over on the cot to make room. "What you got on the box, brother?"

"Got the Temps, blood," Higgins answered, coming off like the skinny white kid he was. With the flip of a switch, "Ain't Too Proud To Beg" came from the tinny speakers.

At once the cleft in Monroe's chin showed with his smile. "Damn right!" he said, glancing at Conroy who had slid to a more comfortable position on the floor. He looked a bit peaked. "You gotta learn to dig this shit, Conroy." With that Monroe jumped to his feet.

Douh shuffled quickly out of his way, nearly tripping over Preacher still reclining on the floor. Monroe gave a little leap, executed a snappy about-face, and slid into a dance step.

Leon struggled to stand and took a position beside Monroe, attempting to mimic the graceful steps.

"See, Conroy? Leon can get with it," Monroe said while they rolled their fists to the beat.

Tucker ignored the goings-on and picked up the bean. First sniffing, then bending it gently.

"What's that?" Higgins asked. His eyebrows arched above the rims of his glasses.

"Vanilla," Tucker said without looking up. He was never quite sure how to talk to Higgins, never sure how much of a conversation Higgins understood.

Douh slipped onto the cot next to Tucker and stared at the

bean with them.

"Vanilla orchid," Douh said, genuinely interested. He hadn't seen one in a long time, not since the North.

"You know these things, Doe-doe?" Tucker said.

The men had quickly picked up on Boyle's moniker for Douh, but he didn't mind. He got along well with most of the men, and felt as if he had an actual friend in Tucker.

"Yes. I've seen them."

"Nice?" Tucker asked.

"Their flowers are small, yellow. Yes. They are right on," Douh said.

"You're saying your dad knows how to grow this stuff?" Tucker asked, once Monroe had settled in across from him.

"He never done it before, but he knows what it takes," Monroe answered with a vacant shrug. He couldn't understand what all the fuss was about. The fact orchids grew in the tropics shouldn't come as a surprise to any of them. "Man, there's most likely orchids growing all over this country," Monroe added.

"But people don't get vanilla by finding wild orchids. They raise them the way they farm anything else, right?" Tucker said.

"Plantations," Monroe offered, finishing off his boiler-maker with a pained expression.

"You see any orchids in the village?" Tucker asked.

"Preach found them beans in those people's shack this morning," Monroe said, his voice momentarily hoarse from the bourbon. "When me an' Conroy come in, they was standing there looking at 'em. Weren't no orchids growing in that village that I could see."

Monroe passed the can in Douh's direction. "You want a pull of this, Doe-doe?"

"No thank you, Monroe." He had trouble pronouncing R's, and always said Monroe and Tucker's names as if they didn't have one.

"Yeah, I don't blame you," Monroe said and took another drink.

"So this is like its seed?" Tucker went on, holding the bean up, examining it from every angle.

"Inside that thing there's a zillion of them. But it's difficult to just plant one and have it grow. Pop says the best way is to get a flower, roots an all. Seems I remember him saying in the wild they sometimes grow on the side of a host tree. Most likely it's where that come from. But orchids are finicky. People spend their lives trying to figure them out."

"So the only reason they're valuable is because that's where vanilla comes from?"

Monroe shook his head with a reflective smile and stared at the candle. "Tucker, my man. Orchids are valuable because of folks like my pop. He ain't the only person ever went ape-shit for the things. Collectors will pay whatever it takes to own a rare one that only a few people have ever seen."

At that moment, Bastard bolted through the doorway, and after two strides, leaped for the center pole of the room. He caught it with four paws and scurried to the top, knocking the belts of M-60 ammo hanging from it to the floor with the sound of a log chain dropping.

A half second later the first mortar arrived, landing a good thirty meters outside the wire.

"Incoming!"

Monroe smashed the light bulb with the butt of Conroy's rifle, while at the same time Douh, Leon, and Tucker hit the floor together. Monroe snuffed the candle on his way down to join them. Higgins had slid to his knees, but he kept looking out the screen.

In the distance, the hollow thump of a round leaving a mortar tube reached them. Seconds later it exploded with a splitting crack inside Charlie Company's area.

"Motherfucker's got it now!" Monroe screamed, fumbling blindly for something to cover his head with.

Leon lay on his stomach, his hands pressed flat against the floor, about to run. "We gotta get to the bunker!"

"I think he's right," Higgins said, though he continued to stare outside.

Two more thunks came from the distance in rapid succession. The third round landed a few meters from the second.

Just that quickly Leon was on his feet and charging for the back door. He stopped long enough to grab one of Preacher's feet, then started backpedaling from the hootch. Monroe followed, doing the same with Conroy. Douh brought up the rear.

"Hey, Tucker," Higgins said, whispering for some reason. "We better get to the bunker, man."

Another round went off. This one sounded as if it had landed past them, in the direction of Headquarters Company. In a moment, a voice screamed for a medic. From the distance another voice called in answer.

Tucker heard nothing but the explosions. Not Higgins. Not the thump of the tube. Not anything. For by now, he had assumed the position. His knees were drawn to his chest, chin tucked between them. Both hands were locked over the back of his neck, clasping so tightly the knuckles turned white. Air entered and left his lungs in shallow gasps, keeping beat with the pounding in his ears.

Higgins crawled beside him. "Tucker! Come on, man! We gotta get—"

A mortar exploded close by the hootch just then, cutting Higgins short. Chunks of shrapnel sizzled up through the screens, ripping holes in the canvas roof on their way out.

Bastard let loose a piercing wail and dropped from the pole. When he hit the floor, he darted underneath the cot and ran dead into Tucker. Without thinking, and in one swift motion, Tucker scooped Bastard into his arms, smothering him to his chest.

The next explosion was so close it bit a chunk of metal from the side of a drum support under the hootch. The room lighted with a brilliant flash, and the floor shook as if hell itself were opening beneath it. Suddenly, Higgins pitched forward, covering Tucker and Bastard.

Heart-pounding moments passed. The generator hummed in the distance. Close by, a frog chirped from a paddy, and then another joined it. Bastard struggled to free himself, but Tucker continued to hold him in a death grip. Around them, men called to each other in the camp, and gradually, Tucker came back to himself. When he released Bastard, the monkey broke for the door and was gone as quickly as he'd come. Only then did Tucker feel Higgins' weight lying over him.

Before Tucker could move, Monroe hurried back into the place with Leon and Douh on his heels. The beam of Monroe's flashlight swung wildly over the room before settling on Tucker's upturned face.

"Higgins is hurt!" Tucker said with a grunt, trying to squirm from beneath the dead weight.

Gently, Monroe and Leon rolled Higgins to his back. Tucker got to his knees with them. Monroe swept the flashlight down Higgins' body. There wasn't any blood. But when the light came to rest on his face they all cringed at the sight of Higgins' nose shoved to a weird angle. A smoldering chunk of wood torn from the hootch floor lay to one side of his head. His shattered glasses on the other.

"He's alive!" Leon shouted. "Higgins! Higgins! You all right, man?"

Higgins' face dropped to the floor beside his glasses, then lifted back up to the light. His eyes worked slowly around their sockets right before he passed out again.

Chapter 13

Sau Ban and Tay Ninh were crawling from the safety of her bunker. The house was dark now, and Sau Ban sat peeking at the camp through the shutters of the back window. A parachute flare ignited in the low sky, its hard glare casting shadows through Charlie Company and a good portion of the village. Light ran through the shutters of Tay Ninh's house and striped the room with gold.

Sau Ban picked up the conversation exactly where it had been left off. "I will need to know when this Douh leaves the camp, Tay Ninh," he said just before the flare drifted into a paddy and everything went black once more.

Tay Ninh said nothing. She was already fumbling in the top drawer of the bureau for her opium pipe. The mortars had frightened her like they always did, and she needed another smoke more than ever.

Sau Ban turned from the window, and he leaned into the stucco wall. In the hopes he might be able to get his hands on Douh, he had changed his plans. He would stay the night. Perhaps Tay Ninh could learn something of interest tomorrow. He was in no hurry. Sau Ban now knew what had become of Douh after he'd failed to return to their safe-house that day. And none of it surprised him. Sau Ban had said as much to his companions the night he abandoned the place himself, feeling there was a good chance their hideout was no longer safe. An opportunity to kill Douh would certainly be worth any delay in his plans.

Sau Ban considered the dark form of Tay Ninh feeding her habit on the other side of the room. The money he'd been able to shake out of the villagers in Xon Dao was far less than he'd hoped. The thought of telling Tay Ninh that he was short the amount she would need to purchase a mortar for him was an embarrassment he would rather forego.

His mind wandered to a youthful memory. Money was easy to come by in those days. Even a young boy could support his mother with nothing more than a quick eye and the nerve to take what was unguarded. There were always men willing to buy the things young boys had to sell. And there were men like the Algerian. The one the Legionnaires called Omar. The one with the winding scar over his black face, the one who gave him gifts, bought him food. The one who followed him, staggering, calling his name on the street one night. Sau Ban could hear the voice, the cooing, cynical sound of it. He could hear the stumbling footsteps coming close behind; smell the panting, greasy breath; feel again the jaw-like grip on his small shoulders, the callused hands, the probing fingers. When Sau Ban could no longer last out against the trapped pressure building in his chest he had screamed. Screamed for the rain to take him away from that dark place, to hide him where it hid the leaves, the brown river. Even now the scream rolled behind his ears, and he slapped them until the house grew quiet once more.

A match flared on the other side of the room, and he watched Tay Ninh touching it to the long-stemmed pipe. Her face lighted in profile, then the match went out, leaving only the glow of the opium ball. A burning red eye on the shallow cup of the pipe.

Chapter 14

During the mortar attack, Clayborn remained in the officer's hootch, shrinking with each explosion, but continuing by flashlight his work on the letter informing Sheila of his decision to leave the Army. Some time back he had decided not to run to the bunker behind the hootch during mortar attacks, and he wasn't sure exactly why. The act of staying where he was, exposed and ready to take what was coming, seemed like the right thing to do. For Clayborn had come to believe in fate. Our numbers are given to us the day we are born. And when that number comes up, all the dodging and ducking in the world won't stop us from being called.

By the time Clayborn finished the letter's final draft, the night had reached its darkest point. Over the bunkers the clouds were thick, low, and full of rain. The guards were at the halfway point of the midnight to dawn watch, and some dozed, some told themselves to stay awake. The artillery battery had been silent most of the night, and the rest of the camp as well. A breeze kicked up from the treelines, blowing steadily over Tan Tru. At that moment the place was as quiet as it ever got.

Clayborn lay back on the cot, his thoughts wandering to the blackness of that night on the canal when Doolin lost his arm. He could hear the sound of frogs in his recollection: their high-pitched droning.

The day had started with such promise. More like some exotic field exercise than anything. This was almost a happy time for Clayborn, this doing what he'd been trained to do. And he felt successful for the first time in his life.

The scenery was lush and thick. The greens were so rich, at times, with the wind and sunlight stirring them to life, the colors of the treelines seemed to pulse.

Conversations began and ended in the middle as RTO's relayed messages throughout the platoon. Laminated maps, pulled from damp leg pockets, crackled stiffly as they were unfolded and checked. Wet boots made plunging sounds with each step when water gushed from ventilation holes in the arch. Many times he thought of Sheila, of what she would think if she could see him here, leading men in combat.

When evening came, the platoon traveled west along the Song Vam Co Tay. And suddenly Clayborn had little idea where he was. Unlike back in the world, there wasn't anything he could orient himself with. No farmhouse in the distance with a security light hanging from a tall pole, no lights of a city or town shaded into the horizon. The men could only see a few feet in front of them, and they moved cautiously, inching their way along narrow paddy dikes, or moving noisily through knee-deep water.

With every step Clayborn forced himself to concentrate on something other than the names of booby-traps: Bouncing Bettys, Toe Poppers, Widow Makers, Daisy Chains. He imagined the trail covered with them. Each time his boot came down he expected an explosion.

He needed to piss but was afraid to call for a halt. Finally, he simply did what he knew all along he would have to do. Clayborn pissed his pants. What was the difference? He was wet from the waist down anyway, what could it matter? Clayborn assured himself it was like pissing in a swimming pool, and doing it gave him the same giddy feeling of excitement. What would Sheila think about this? He saw himself at home, telling her stories of the war, of men pissing themselves because it was too dark to stop.

A noise behind him soon brought his thoughts back to matters at hand. A rattle came from his rucksack. A tiny tick of metal on metal. What the hell was it? He hadn't heard it during the daytime, but now something sounded with each step. The noise grew in Clayborn's mind until it rang like a cowbell. He tried shifting the ruck on his shoulders and stumbled into Heavy, the platoon's RTO, who had stopped walking when the platoon did.

"Pardon me," Clayborn said, as one foot slipped from the dike and into the paddy with a loud splash. Apologizing was a ridiculous thing to do, as if the two of them had bumped into each other on the street somewhere. And Heavy drew his face close to Clayborn's. "You're excused," he said, and he snorted softly through his nose.

The platoon had covered a little over three hundred meters when Sergeant Drieser, walking slack behind Burdick on point, brought them to a halt. They had arrived at their destination for the night: the junction between the river and a canal.

Without talking it over with Clayborn, Drieser sent word that the platoon should string out along the river. From there they could watch for sampans coming or going either way. The nipa palm that lined the riverbank was over their heads by several feet, and the men rustled into the thickness of it, then all was quiet once more.

Clayborn said nothing until everyone was in place. He then sent word that he would like to speak with Drieser. A minute later, Drieser appeared out of the darkness so suddenly it startled Clayborn.

Drieser crouched next to him, his face close enough that Clayborn could smell paddy water and sweat. After a brief whispered discussion between them—and at Clayborn's insistence—Drieser agreed to send some men up the canal as a precaution.

Clayborn had given his first order of the day, and felt it a good one.

That's when the frogs started. In the distance their chirping rose in a loud chorus to a high decibel, then stopped, only to start again. Clayborn began counting the seconds between chorus and silence, while Heavy sat next to him, the handset pressed to his ear.

After a few minutes, four figures stepped out of the nipa palm and moved in line beside the canal. Immediately the frogs stopped chirping, and the soft rustle of men and equipment was the only sound. Clayborn strained his eyes from behind a palm frond, but could see little.

In another minute Drieser slipped through the vegetation and crouched in front of Clayborn. "I'll need to be here with your radio, Lieutenant, the men have mine," he whispered, sitting on the other side of Heavy, and the three of them closed in tightly.

Just then a hole opened in the cloud cover, and starlight lit the darkness.

Doolin took the point, followed by Burdick, Conroy and Monroe. From where Clayborn sat, the men appeared as one large shadow gliding quietly beside the canal's thick stands of nipa palm.

Every few feet Doolin stopped, waiting and listening, before moving on. In a few minutes the men crept out of sight around a bend in the canal and were gone.

To pass time while Heavy waited for word that the men were in position, Clayborn stared at the sky. This close to the equator more stars were visible than he had ever seen in his life. He'd taken an astronomy class in college, but had only done enough work to get a passing grade. There were eighty-eight constellations, he remembered that much, but as to the ones he might be seeing, he didn't have a clue. He made a mental note to ask Sheila to send him a map of the celestial bodies. If nothing else, she would like the fact he was trying to improve himself.

Squelch broke on the radio's handset and Clayborn's thoughts returned to the matters at hand. He moved his head closer to Heavy's, hoping to catch what was being said. Heavy passed the horn to Drieser and Clayborn moved so close his nose bumped into the side of Heavy's face.

"They've got movement ahead of them on the canal, Lieutenant," Drieser whispered.

There was more squelch, and Drieser pressed the horn to his ear quickly. "They want to know what to do."

Before Clayborn could say anything, Drieser keyed the handset and spoke slowly. "Pull back and return to our position. Over."

Drieser kept the horn to his ear and leaned across Heavy. "They've seen two Victor Charlies."

"Repeat. Return to our position," Drieser said.

The first crack of automatic weapons fire broke the stillness so suddenly that for an instant Clayborn imagined seeing a rip in the blackness around him. Green and red tracers sprayed over the canal, ricocheting like sparks from a grindstone. And Clayborn felt frozen in time, awestruck at the colorful display. By the time he recovered his thinking and became aware of the magnitude of what was taking place, the firefight had ended.

The silence that followed was broken when someone moaned so low that Clayborn thought it might be the wind. His thumb fiddled with his rifle's safety, and he stared up the canal. To the left and right of him men stirred along the river. His thumb felt for the safety again, flicked it off and on nervously. Adrenaline surged to the point of making him light-headed. Clayborn had the sensation of standing outside himself, watching, but unable to change any of it.

Drieser keyed the handset. "Pull back. Get out of there now. Pull back."

Yes. Make them stop, Clayborn had thought. He wanted to stand up and wave the moment away like he could in training. All right. I screwed this up. Everyone get back to their original positions. We're going to try it again.

Squelch, and this time the voice over the horn was loud enough that Clayborn could hear words, but couldn't make out what was being said.

The smell of cordite drifted in like a slow fog, so thick that Clayborn could taste it. He realized he'd been breathing hard. There was a wad of spit in the back of his throat he couldn't seem to swallow.

"We need a dust-off," Drieser said, handing the horn back to Heavy. He crouched in front of Clayborn and spoke in a normal voice. "We have wounded, Lieutenant." Drieser then hustled away.

Clayborn's eyes rolled the way a man's will when he finds out he's been the butt of an ongoing joke.

Drieser's voice came from somewhere to the right of him, calling for Doc, Leon and Preacher. In short order, Drieser and the men stepped from the nipa palm in single file. They moved now without regard for noise. Soon they disappeared around the turn. A few more seconds and Clayborn heard them make contact with the LP. No one whispered anymore, and from the way the sound carried in the night, they could have been only a few meters away. Beside him Heavy repeated coordinates to the dust-off pilot who was leaving the hospital unit at Can Tho.

There was a pause in the activity just then, and Clayborn heard what sounded to him like the mewing of a cat. He was having a difficult time controlling his thinking. His mind seemed to be cleansing itself of thought so quickly that he couldn't hold an idea for more than an instant. His bladder suddenly felt filled to the point of bursting. He turned sharply on his knees and fumbled with his pants. Piss ran down the inside of his leg.

Heavy stood and peered to the south. Clayborn listened for the thump of the chopper. He could hear something but wasn't sure if it was blood pounding in his ears, the bite of rotor blades, or what. Why couldn't everything just slow down a bit and let him catch up? He felt about ten seconds behind the situation. Each time he thought of a plan of action, Heavy or Drieser had already performed it.

Heavy spoke to the medevac pilot over the radio and a light beamed in the sky far to the south, then vanished.

Finally, the chopper hovered to a landing, the beam of its belly light sweeping the area below, illuminating the dust and dead vegetation kicked up by its rotors. Men scurried in a crouch below the blades, loading someone aboard, then just as quickly, the chopper lifted back into the sky and was gone. The silence that followed hurt Clayborn's ears.

After a while, Drieser radioed that he would maintain his present position on the canal, and the rest of the night passed without incident, but Clayborn didn't sleep. The frogs wouldn't let him.

In the morning the platoon seemed filled with a nervous energy that hadn't been there the day before. The men were quiet, solemn, and none would make eye contact with him.

The rest of the platoon was finishing their breakfasts, preparing to move out, and Clayborn was kneeling alone over his map. When he looked up, Tucker Burdick was standing over him, holding something that Clayborn's mind refused to register. He remembered smiling, sure that this must be some kind of trick the men were playing on him. Without a word Burdick dropped Doolin's severed arm in front of him and walked away.

Clayborn couldn't move, nor could he pull his eyes away from the arm. The fingers of Doolin's hand were spread wide, the arm was bent slightly at the elbow, and shattered bone poked from the torn pink muscle. Clayborn had cried that morning, but there were no tears. His emotions seemed unwilling to release themselves. Finally, he vomited, again and again until there was nothing more to give. He understood his stupidity had changed a young man's life forever. He knew it had changed his own as well. And once Sheila received his letter, she would know it, too. He rolled to his side on the cot, both hands sandwiched between his knees, and fell to sleep. His ears filled with the sound of frogs.

Chapter 15

All morning it looked like rain. But by noon the sun burned through the clouds, searing the air around OP-4 with a torrid brilliance that drew moisture from the paddies in shimmering curtains. So far the day was windless, and the distant treelines were calm as a picture.

The OP sat to the side of the road on a elevated mound of hard mud, and at that moment Monroe knelt beside the radio, an olive-drab towel draped over his head. The muscles of his arms flexed while he twisted a P-38 can opener around the top of a C-ration.

Leon watched from the other side of the radio. He wore his boonie hat low over his eyes and concentrated on a bead of sweat he could feel running inside his flak vest. Tucker sat at their feet, smoking, his head and back bare, his eyes watching up the road where someone rode a bicycle in their direction.

In a few minutes an elderly man stopped his bike in front of them, smiling from beneath the brim of a pith helmet that was soiled a permanent gray. The old man wore a pair of orange shorts made from the nylon fabric of a large parachute flare. When he motioned with two fingers held to his lips, Leon waved him in.

"Cigalet, you?" the old man said, nodding and smiling at Leon, closing the short distance between them.

"Yeah, papasan. Cigalet, me."

Leon tossed him a Marlboro with one hand, offering him a light with the other.

"Numba one," the man said, examining the cigarette like a connoisseur before holding the filter to his lips.

For a spell, no one had anything to say, and the four of them sat there quietly, each lost in his thoughts.

Leon's gaze wandered to Tucker, who had his knees drawn up, his arms hanging loosely over them. He'd taken his flak vest off earlier, and Leon saw there was an infected pimple on the middle of his back. He wondered if Tucker knew it was there, but didn't ask.

Finally, Tucker said: "I keep thinking about those orchids, Monroe."

"Oh, man, forget that shit," Monroe said, lighting a smoke of his own.

The old man duck-walked to where Monroe sat, motioning to his lips once more. Monroe shook a Salem loose, and Papasan took it with a grin.

Tucker flashed his lighter beside the old man's face. "Think about it. How often does somebody get what they really want?"

"Most folks lucky to get what they need, Tucker. Forget it, my man."

Tucker tossed a clump of dirt over the road, then glanced in either direction. "Look at this place. We been here what—?"

"Three-hundred-thirty-three days," Leon finished for him.

"Yeah," Tucker said. "And ain't no good going to come of any of it."

"We get ourselves home in one piece, some good sure as shit going to come of it," Monroe offered.

"That isn't what I mean." Tucker scooted around to face them. "This place," he waved both arms wide, "none of it makes sense, right?"

"Ain't no lie," Monroe answered, and Leon nodded. The old man stared past them and smoked contentedly, his eyes closed under the brim of the helmet.

"Then what's so crazy about wanting to get your dad his orchid?"

"Nothing, except for the fact we don't know where any are."

Monroe let the cigarette dangle from his mouth while he rummaged in his rucksack. A second later he produced a can of Kiwi polish and brush, then began smearing the black polish over the weathered toes and heels of his jungle boots.

Leon pressed his back into the rim of the embankment, cleaning a filthy fingernail with the tip of his bayonet.

"Be easy enough to find out," Tucker said, and looked far down the road where a cloud of orange dust signaled something large coming from the direction of Highway 4.

Monroe grunted, picking up the brush, buffing the toe of a boot. "Be easy enough to get shot trying, too."

Leon kept quiet. At the time he was examining the frazzled toes of his own boots. If anyone understood how single-minded Tucker could be, it was Leon. But he also knew there was little chance Tucker would drop the subject without debate, and he wanted to stay out of it.

"Just listen." Tucker straightened his posture a bit. "Christmas is next week—"

"And that ain't nothing but one more day in the Nam," Monroe said.

Tucker ignored the comment. "Rumor has it there's going to be a three day cease-fire."

"I know," Monroe added quickly. "And that's going to be three days of sleep." He gave up on the boots, stuffing everything back in the ruck, then leaned into the embankment and lit another smoke.

"That would be the perfect time to go for them orchids."

"You're crazy, Tucker. You know that?" Monroe said. The towel hung so far over his face that only the cigarette could be seen poking from it. "What we gonna do, tell Top and everybody that we wanna split for a few days to pick flowers?"

Leon snickered at this, and Tucker shot him a look.

"I don't have that part figured out yet. But we could do it. . .if we wanted to."

In a few minutes a deuce-and-a-half emerged from the cloud of dust Tucker had seen earlier, and a short while later, the truck came speeding by with eight men dressed in new fatigues riding in the back. The FNG's waved at the OP on their way past. Tucker, Leon, and Monroe only watched. The old man used the break in the conversation to shuffle closer to Tucker, and he bummed another smoke.

"Sorry bastards," Monroe said, watching the truck rumble on up the road. He pulled the towel over his face when the dust began to settle over the OP.

Tucker watched the old man puff on the cigarette. "This guy has been out here before."

"Hell yes," Monroe answered from behind the towel. "How else would he get his smokes?"

"Look at him." Tucker tapped Monroe's knee. "Look how happy he is."

Monroe peeked with one eye at the man. The guy looked content, all right. "Yeah. What of it?"

Tucker got to his feet. "He gets a lousy cigarette and the old boy thinks everything is number one." He paced back and forth for a few seconds before squatting in front of Monroe and Leon. "We got the chance to get your dad a rare orchid, and all you're worried about is catching up on sleep."

"Ain't nobody said it was rare, Tucker."

"But what if it was? What if the thing was one people had never seen before?"

"Then it would be worth having," Monroe said, but added: "So what? By the time my pop got the thing it wouldn't be worth shit."

"You sure about that?"

"Damn, Tucker. It takes five days for a letter to get home, more for a package. Any orchid gonna be long gone by the time it get back to the world."

"But that's the flower. What about the roots? What if we dug up the roots, kept them in their original soil, wrapped it all up. Then your dad might have something."

"The climate, Tucker. The man don't have the right climate."

"Maybe a wild orchid is different. . .stronger, or something?"

Monroe's face took on a thoughtful expression. "Maybe."

"Your dad knows about these things. If anybody could get it to grow again, he could, right?"

"I ain't so sure about that, Tucker."

"Can't you picture his face when he opened the package?"

Monroe squinted up the road, then his gaze softened when he turned it on Tucker. "Damn, man, let's quit talking about home."

"My dad never wanted nothing in his life. Not a job, not my mother. Nothing! Nothing but another drink. Ask Leon what my old man is," Tucker said, motioning with his head. "He'll tell you."

Monroe glanced in Leon's direction, but Leon looked away.

"See? You ask anybody back home about my father and they can't look at you either." Tucker stood once more and stared across the paddies, his arms folded.

The sun seemed brighter to Leon's eyes, as if the moment required better light. Suddenly a gust of humid wind tipped the pith helmet on the old man's head and he pressed it down with one hand. From far off, the faint thump of chopper blades reached the OP.

"Do you remember how it was, Leon?" Tucker asked, facing him.

"How what was?"

"How it was before we came here. Can you remember that?"

Leon peeked at his friend. Sunlight streaked his brown hair with strands of blonde. Smile lines arched from his nostrils to the corners of his mouth. Shadowed by the sun, the lines appeared deep, and unused.

Tucker moved closer. "Answer my question. Do you remember how it was?"

"You mean at home?"

"Yeah."

"It was like. . .home, man. It was the same for both of us."

"No, Leon. It wasn't the same for both of us. After school you went home to your parents. Your mom would have supper going, your dad would be reading the paper. Am I right?"

Leon could only nod.

"Tell Monroe what I did."

Leon glanced at Monroe, then down at the ground, but said nothing.

"You ever seen a man with the DT's, Monroe?"

The towel slipped from Monroe's head. "I guess not."

"You know what they are?"

"Yeah. Something that happens to . . ."

"Drunks," Tucker finished for him. "The first time I seen my father with the DT's, he stumbled into my room howling like a dog." Tucker paused and squatted on his haunches, and spoke like he was thinking out loud. "Bugs crawling on him, on the ceiling and walls. Then snakes, snakes everywhere in the house. He howled all night."

Tucker ran his gaze over the two of them like he'd forgotten they were there. "That's what I got to go home to. And I'm telling you right now that if you don't want to get your dad his orchid, then I'll do it myself."

Monroe and Leon exchanged looks, and it grew quiet. To the west, five choppers flew like large dragonflies in single file above a far treeline.

"Sometimes it feels like we been doing this all our lives." Tucker said.

"Know what bothers me?" Tucker went on. "The other day I realized that home really ain't there anymore. Not like it used to be."

"Ain't sure what you mean, Tuck," Leon said.

"You remember the night Connie Doolin lost his arm?"

"Yeah."

"Well, he went home, but home ain't gonna be the way it was. See what I mean?"

"He's alive, though."

"I keep thinking that some day I might run into him and he's going to ask about his ring," Tucker said.

"That ain't going to happen."

"I didn't do nothing with it. It's still there. I buried it all."

"It was okay, Tuck."

"Now and then I wonder if maybe I should have tried to get it off. I could have sent it to him or something, you know?"

"You did the right thing, Tuck. Doolin probably don't even think about it."

Before anyone could say more, the old man got to his feet. He pressed his hands together and bowed, then hurried to his bike and rode away.

Tucker rubbed both hands over his face, then shifted his eyes in the direction the old man had gone. "Maybe you're right, Monroe. Maybe the whole thing is crazy."

Monroe mopped the towel beneath his chin thoughtfully, then arranged it back over the top of his bald head.

"How you figure we could do it?" Monroe said, then added quickly: "Just for the hell of it, mind you."

Tucker continued to stare up the road. When he turned around, his lips wore a tight grin.

Leon didn't like it. He knew once Tucker got rolling with his plan there would be no turning back. If Tucker could convince Monroe, the two of them would drag the rest of the squad into the scheme, and him with it.

"Don't get him started, Monroe," Leon said. "Just drop it all right now."

Monroe drew back a corner of the towel and peeked at Leon. "Ain't no harm in hearing what the man got to say. Go on, Tucker. How you figure to do it, my man?"

Chapter 16

Clayborn and the rest of the squad, including, Sergeant Drieser and Heavy, had been waiting at the river for over an hour. The evening sky had turned a dirty gray. Behind them the camp was fast becoming a washed-out silhouette in the dim light. The men spoke in hushed tones, listening for the first low rumbles of the LST boat coming up the Song Vam Co Tay to get them.

Sau Ban had spent the day in Tay Ninh's house, waiting for her to return from work. He knew what he'd asked her to do would be difficult. The chance Douh might be privy to advance information on the comings and goings of the unit was slim at best. So when Tay Ninh arrived back home at the end of the day, Sau Ban wasn't surprised that she had nothing new to report.

But there had to be a way, and he'd spent the hours brooding on Douh and peeking through the back window at the camp. Once he thought he saw Douh walking beside a bunker, but couldn't be sure. Maybe he could wait at the window with a rifle, hoping for a clear shot at the traitor before escaping down the tunnel. But that would mean exposing Tay Ninh, and her usefulness, to the Americans. It would also mean that Sau Ban wouldn't have the pleasure of seeing the look on Douh's face when he killed him. He decided to give it time. There was plenty of that. Maybe something would come up.

As daylight faded over the camp, Sau Ban made himself ready to leave. He told Tay Ninh he was going back to the forest. She was to keep her ears open for anything helpful, and he would be returning in a few days with one of his men. In the meantime, Tay Ninh should arrange for the purchase of an American mortar tube and as many rounds as possible to go with it. The next time he visited, Sau Ban assured her, he would have the money.

Like always, the trip through the tunnel passed with the sense of blind confinement. By the time Sau Ban shinnied up the walls of the exit pit and peeked out, the last edge of twilight was drifting from the area.

Douh waited by the river with the rest of the squad. He needed to urinate. He could have urinated right there, but was shy about these things and preferred privacy.

Douh stepped around the edge of the nipa palm and unzipped his fatigues. He heard something and at first thought it only the wind. But no, he could hear breathing. When Douh looked into the growing darkness of the foliage for the source of the sound, Sau Ban's face was staring back, his body hidden behind the dense palms. He was near enough that had Douh taken a few more steps he could have touched him. A scream caught in Douh's throat, and then, like a dream, Sau Ban's image withdrew behind the darkness. A moment later the nipa palm rustled for a few seconds and then grew still.

Douh felt a sharp pain in his groin and realized he was gripping himself so hard it hurt. For a while it was impossible to move. His heart rattled in his chest, and he breathed like he'd been running in sunshine. How had Sau Ban known where to find him? Douh couldn't say, and realized it didn't matter. His stomach felt filled with ice water. His knees shook.

By the time Douh composed himself enough to return, the LST was making its way around a bend in the river and the men were saddling up.

Douh didn't mention the encounter with Sau Ban. What would he say? That while urinating he had seen the face of someone he knew standing in the jungle? No one would believe him, and Douh couldn't blame them for that. He had enough problems without the men thinking him hysterical. To his way of thinking, the fact that Sau Ban had found him already made things about as bad as they could get.

Part Two

Chapter 17

The rumor of a Christmas cease-fire proved true. Beginning at 12:01 on December 24th, all hostilities—at least on paper—were to be suspended until midnight of the 26th. The first leg of Tucker's plan had fallen into place.

It had taken some time to convince Preacher, and though he wasn't too fond of the idea, he finally agreed to throw his lot in with them. The way Monroe described how the orchids—if indeed they found any—would be growing high up the sides of trees sparked Preacher's curiosity to see them. And it wasn't like the squad was made up of a bunch of rear echelons. The soldiers had worked in the area of Xon Dao on more than one occasion. With the cease-fire in place, the men wouldn't be looking for trouble, and Tucker assured everyone that contact with the enemy would be avoided if at all possible. They'd learned how to stay out of trouble if they wanted to.

But the second part of the plan—how to get away in the first place—proved to be a little more difficult. They couldn't just saunter out of the camp in broad daylight without someone wanting to know where they thought they were going; nor could they slip out at night without first clearing their departure so they weren't shot by their own troops. But then, even that problem solved itself, and it came from an unlikely source. Lieutenant Clayborn.

Clayborn asked for volunteers for a listening post a short distance outside the camp's perimeter the evening of the 23rd. The camp still needed night security, cease-fire or not, but because of the season, Clayborn hoped he wouldn't have to pick the men himself. It would be the only LP they would pull during the three-day stand-down, he promised, and so he wasn't surprised when Tucker and the squad offered their services.

On the morning of the 23rd, word reached the camp that an

ARVN unit had stepped in the shit somewhere on the Cambodian border. Charlie Company had been slated to work in conjunction with the Riverine boats for the day. Instead, the company was placed on alert to act as a reactionary force if the ARVN's needed them. The men were confined to the company area to wait, and Boyle saw to it that boredom didn't have a chance to set in. There were sandbags to be filled, bunkers that needed shoring up, and of course the latrine's waste tubs could always use a good burning.

Boyle, hoping to rid the latrine of the shithouse fly, had placed a fifty-dollar bounty on the pest. He'd even ordered the tubs burned twice a day in case the fat thing could be caught napping in one of them. But nothing had worked, and the fly continued to enjoy the comforts of home.

While 2nd squad went about their chores, they talked among themselves, each offering his opinion as to what would be needed for the trip. They should travel as lightly as possible, Tucker said, running down a checklist of what the men should bring. Two days rations ought to do it, he thought. Tucker was counting on one day there, and another back. Maybe they could wrap the thing up in a day. Who could tell? Everything depended on how far they had to go for the orchids. At the most, he told them, they would surely be back in time to eat a hot Christmas dinner with the rest of the company. Everyone needed to carry at least two-hundred rounds of ammo, a couple of grenades, and though Leon argued for claymores, the M-60 machine gun and a LAW rocket launcher, he was voted down. The heaviest piece of equipment would be the radio that they would only use if necessary. Preacher volunteered to be RTO.

Boyle had given sandbag detail to 2nd squad, and the men worked, stripped to the waist, filling and stacking the heavy bags in the afternoon sun.

"How we gonna get away from Clayborn?" Monroe asked, holding a bag out for Tucker to fill. "He gonna be with us on the LP, you know."

"We leave him," Tucker said, not missing a beat.

"Leave him?"

Tucker had the blade of the entrenching tool adjusted to a right angle and he swung the pick side of it into the hard dirt. "We wait until he's sleeping, then we head out."

"But that's like desertion or something, ain't it?" Leon asked.

"We ain't deserting nothing, Leon," Tucker said, giving him a sharp look."Hell, we can leave him a note if you want. He'll be fine. The camp's right behind him."

"Drieser gonna be pissed," Monroe said.

Tucker didn't have an answer for that, so he kept quiet and swung the shovel.

"You forgetting something else, Tucker," Monroe said.

Tucker stopped in mid-swing and looked at him.

"How we gonna find out from them people where the orchids are?"

"See, we're screwed right there," Leon chimed in.

The shovel slammed into the dirt."We're taking Douh with us."

"He know what we're up to?" Monroe asked.

"I already talked to him," Tucker said.

"Of course," Leon muttered under his breath.

Monroe lit a cigarette and exhaled a loud stream of smoke through his lips."I guess that about does it, then, don't it?"

Tucker nodded.

Just then Preacher and Conroy showed up, each with an armload of empty bags.

"Top says if we run out, there's more where these came from," Preacher announced, and he dropped his bundle at their feet.

Douh spent the day hiding from Boyle and waiting for afternoon when Tay Ninh would be returning with the soldier's laundry. Laundry day was always a good excuse to visit Tay Ninh, and this time Douh was determined to carry on a conversation with her. But he tried to keep his mind on other things. Thinking of Tay Ninh always gave Douh an erection. He couldn't very well stand in front of Tay Ninh, rigid as a tent stake.

At 1500, Douh saw Tay Ninh pulling her laundry-cart through the company area. With an eye out for Boyle, he darted from the bunker he'd been hiding behind and ducked into the laundry shack.

When Tay Ninh came through the back door a few minutes later, Douh stood grinning at her from the other side of the counter.

"Good afternoon, Tay Ninh," he said. His eyes seemed to have a mind of their own, and he had to force them to remain on her.

Tay Ninh brushed a strand of hair from her face. "Good afternoon, Douh," she said, bowing slightly.

Douh looked past her at the stack of laundry outside her door. Because it was easier than thinking of something to say, he scooted under the counter and hurried to the door, grabbing bundles of fatigues and rushing back in with them.

In a few minutes all the bundles were lying here and there about the floor, and an uneasy quiet fell over the room.

Tay Ninh was the first to speak. "It will take me a while to find your clothes, Douh," she smiled. "I hope you won't mind waiting?"

Douh imagined how her long lashes would feel touching his cheek.

"No, Tay Ninh. I do not mind at all," he said.

"Why not sit while you wait," she said, and motioned at a stool behind him.

Tay Ninh squatted among the bundles of laundry, and began to organize them into stacks.

"The Americans must be feeling happy with their coming celebration, Douh."

He loved the way she said his name, how her voice rose at the end of it. "Yes . . . some of them."

"Only some, Douh?" she asked. "I would think that three days with nothing to do would make everyone happy."

Her long delicate fingers smoothed hair back from her face. It splayed over her shoulders like a lovely shawl. Douh wanted to pull her to him, bury his face in that hair, to smell it, the strands sliding over his lips. With Tay Ninh's back to him it was easier to talk, and he carried on the conversation.

"Not everyone has the time off, Tay Ninh."

"But I thought a cease-fire was for all?"

"It is," Douh said. "But I am going out with some of the men on a special mission." He liked the sound of that, and in fact had chosen the words carefully.

"I hope it is not dangerous," Tay Ninh said. The stacks of laundry were now shuffled into an orderly arrangement around her.

"I do not think so, Tay Ninh."

Douh hoped it wasn't his imagination, but she sounded like she cared.

"But a special mission sounds dangerous. Are you sure?" Tay Ninh turned on the balls of her feet, and rested on her haunches.

She looked up at him. Douh's laundry bundle cradled between her chest and knees.

Douh could smell her, a sweet wavering scent in the stale room.

"We are only going to visit a village and return. It is nothing," he said.

"That depends on the village. Not all are as safe as Tan Tru."

"Yes, Tay Ninh, but we are not looking for the VC. The men only want to ask a question of the villagers."

"How odd," she said, with a curious smile.

Tay Ninh knelt closer and placed the bundle in his lap. Her fingers rested in place for a moment, the backs of them touching his thighs. Douh felt himself growing hard, and swallowed so loudly he thought she might have heard.

"What village are the soldiers so interested in, Douh?" She withdrew her fingers slowly and the bundle settled down on his erection.

Douh couldn't find his voice. When he opened his mouth a small gasp left it that embarrassed him. "Xon Dao. The name of the village is Xon Dao."

"And the men are planning this over their holiday?"

"Yes," he said, still able to feel her hand on his thighs. She was close enough for him to see his own tiny reflection in her eyes.

"The thong miao are strange people. Don't you agree?" Tay Ninh didn't say it as much as she chirped it, and Douh caught himself leaning forward, wanting to get closer to the sound. But as luck would have it, just then, a soldier Douh didn't know stepped through the front door, and Tay Ninh turned away to fetch the man's laundry.

When the soldier had gone, Tay Ninh waved a hand at the bundles of fatigues. "More soldiers will be coming, Douh. I have work to do."

Disappointed, Douh ducked beneath the counter. He was nearly to the door when Tay Ninh stopped him.

"Will you come and see me again?"

Douh's cheeks grew warm. "I would like that very much, Tay Ninh."

"Be careful on your special mission. When you get back I would like to hear all about it."

Douh nearly stepped into the door frame on his way out, and it was all he could do to keep from running once he was outside. But his elation didn't last for long. Boyle spotted him, and after telling him to wipe the smile off his face, and a lecture about malingering, sent him to fill sandbags with the rest of the squad.

Chapter 18

Leon glanced at the sun. It hung low in the sky, taking with it a portion of the fierce heat the men had been working in. Fresh sandbags, ready for hauling to any bunker that needed them were heaped in piles around the men.

"If we want hot chow we better get moving," Leon said.

Hearing this, Douh dropped the entrenching tool and stared at the blisters on both hands. Like a fool he'd offered to spell Tucker with the digging, and now wished he hadn't. He couldn't open or close his palms without pain.

Tucker wiped a hand through the mixture of sweat and dirt on his stomach. He stared down at the tattoo on his chest. Though he'd tried to be careful, it was impossible to keep the thing clean, so he wasn't surprised to see a few tiny beads of pus oozing from beneath the thin scab.

Without anything more being said, the men shuffled off in the direction of the mess hall.

"We got to think of a name," Monroe said over his shoulder at the head of the column.

"Name?" Preacher asked.

"The orchid, my man." Monroe answered, and his voice sounded jaunty.

The more thought Monroe gave to Tucker's plan, the more he'd warmed to the idea, despite the fact the village sat on the edge of the Plain of Reeds. Indian Country is what the men called the Reeds. An area of low swamp, biting insects, leeches, and herds of wild water buffalo. The VC controlled the Plain of Reeds and everyone knew it. The company had never waded in there without something bad happening. 2nd platoon had lost a couple of guys there just last week, and it's where Doolin gave up his arm, and Pearl his legs. But Monroe guessed even Tucker wouldn't try and talk the men into the Reeds, no matter how bad he wanted the orchids.

"If we find any orchids we get to name them," Monroe went on. "Folks do that when they discover a new kind."

He rounded a bend in the path and looked up ahead to where the chow line snaked out of the mess hall's door.

"What if they ain't new?" Preacher asked.

"We won't know that until my pop gets his hands on one. Which reminds me. Make sure you bring your camera, Preach. If them things are in bloom when we get there, I want a picture of it. Might be the only way my old man ever gonna see what the flowers look like. But we gonna name 'em just the same. He'll get a kick outa that if nothing else."

"How about naming them after the village?" Conroy said, his voice breaking halfway through the question.

"Good, Conroy, but too ordinary," Monroe said.

"Mekong Delight," Leon offered.

"That sounds like ice cream, Leon," Tucker said, though he couldn't come up with anything better.

"Goddess of Tan Tru," Douh said, suddenly giving name to a poem he'd been composing in his head since the conversation with Tay Ninh. If he could screw up his courage he would recite it to her on his next visit.

Monroe stopped at the end of the chow line and stared into the distance. "Goddess of Tan Tru. I like it." The cleft of his chin showed when he smiled at Douh. "Right on, Doe-doe. We gonna find us the Sweet Goddess of Tan Tru."

Later that same evening, under cover of darkness, Sau Ban led Tuan along the bank of the Vam Co Tay to the tunnel entrance. In no time they were in the pit, and after leaving their rifles there they began crawling for Tay Ninh's house. Sau Ban was glad to have someone in the tunnel with him, though of course he didn't say as much. He'd only brought Tuan along to help carry the mortar tube Tay Ninh would have purchased by now.

When they were past the halfway point, Sau Ban suddenly felt a rush of fresh air. With some difficulty he rolled to his back and was shocked to find himself looking up at the stars through a hole as large as his head in the ceiling. The constant vibration of artillery was slowly destroying the old tunnel.

For tense moments Sau Ban waited, expecting at any minute to see a rifle barrel poke through the opening. But nothing happened. Only the muffled sound of voices that sounded far off. A second later the earth vibrated. Tuan lay at Sau Ban's feet, crying out with each new blast until Sau Ban kicked him hard on the top of his head and told him to keep quiet. When the short artillery barrage ended, Sau Ban couldn't resist the temptation to look. He wiggled his head through the hole until his face was above ground. The light of the camp seemed brighter than it really was, but even then he still couldn't see farther than a few feet. Piles of empty wooden artillery crates were scattered around the opening. Suddenly Sau Ban heard footsteps and ducked his head back into the tunnel. A second later and an empty crate crashed next to the hole, knocking more of the ceiling onto him. Sau Ban reached up and eased the crate over the gaping hole. Then, with Tuan bumping his heels, they scrambled on for Tay Ninh's.

Like before, the radio played from inside Tay Ninh's home when they arrived at the exit pit. But this time there wasn't any light shining through the floor boards. Not knowing exactly when Sau Ban would be returning, Tay Ninh had kept the bureau in place to cover the trap door.

Sau Ban pressed his ear to the wood and listened for voices. He heard nothing but the blabbering of a radio announcer. He knocked twice, and twice again. Then the bureau grated slowly over the floor, and an instant later Sau Ban poked his head into the room.

Tay Ninh stood back and watched as the two men climbed from the pit. "How nice," she said without smiling. "Two ground hogs have come to visit."

Sau Ban recoiled at this. Being talked down to by Tay Ninh when they were alone was one thing, but in front of Tuan it was unacceptable. His patience with her smart mouth, with using the tunnel to get what he wanted, was all wearing thin. But the time for verbal sparring with Tay Ninh was growing to a close. After seeing how the tunnel had deteriorated, he had thought to tell her of the danger it presented, but now decided to keep it to himself. Soon, the Americans would discover her tunnel, and when they did it would mean the end of their partnership. If she had the information on Douh he wanted, then there would be no need for him to take her insults any longer.

Tuan moved self-consciously about the room. He had never been inside a house with a wooden floor, nor one made of anything but palm fronds. Because Sau Ban didn't tell him otherwise, he took a position next to a wall and squatted in the shadows there.

Sau Ban carried the lamp from the bureau and placed it on the table where he and Tay Ninh settled into chairs. The first order of business was the mortar, and yes, it was there, hidden in the back of her bunker: five rounds to go with it.

"Excellent, Tay Ninh," Sau Ban said. He was genuinely pleased. "And Douh?"

Tay Ninh took her time answering, and Sau Ban used the moment to admire her. Her delicate skin was the color of alabaster in the glow of the lamp.

"All in good time, Sau Ban," Tay Ninh answered. "You haven't yet paid me for the mortar you wanted so badly." She gazed in a distracted way across the room, then back to Sau Ban. "You aren't planning to cheat me, are you?"

Tuan shifted on the balls of his feet, and pressed himself into the wall. Her words made him nervous at the thought of Sau Ban's reaction. He didn't have long to wait.

"Why would I want to cheat you, Tay Ninh?" Sau Ban said through a forced laugh. He had reached his limit with her. There was a pause, then his arm lashed out, striking her, and the sound was like a cupped hand being slapped on water. The blow knocked her sideways from the chair. Tay Ninh's eyes blinked like grit had suddenly been blown into them.

"Now!" he snapped. "Sit down and tell me what I want to know!"

Tay Ninh held her hand on her cheek. Her left eye teared, the wet lash glistened in the lamp light.

"That's better," Sau Ban said, once she had arranged herself on the chair. He peeked over his shoulder to see where Tuan was.

When he turned back to Tay Ninh, her head was bowed, her eyes stared down at the table. He'd never met a woman yet who didn't learn her place after a good cuff on the head. And while he watched her, he told himself he should have done it sooner.

"What do you know of Douh?"

She dropped her hand to the table and Sau Ban could see the flushed outline of his fingers on her cheek.

Tay Ninh kept her eyes lowered, but a defiant tone remained in her voice. "You must pay—"

She didn't get to finish. Sau Ban's arm snapped forward, this time slapping her in the mouth hard enough to draw blood. Tay Ninh fell backward, the chair crashing to the floor with her.

Sau Ban sprang to his feet and took a menacing step toward her, then stopped. "Tuan! Get Tay Ninh's gift from the bunker!"

Tuan quickly did as ordered, and Sau Ban pointed at the mortar tube without taking his eyes from Tay Ninh. "Take it back to the river and wait for me there."

When Tuan hesitated, Sau Ban turned on him, pushing him to the pit and shoving him into it. "Do as I say!" he said, and swatted him on the side of the head for emphasis.

Tuan quickly slid into the tunnel and was gone.

Sau Ban returned and stood over Tay Ninh, a hateful smile on his broad face. "You arrogant bitch!"

He reached down and jerked her to her feet as though she were a small child. His face drew close to hers until he could smell her breath, could hear her shallow breathing, the frightened sound of it.

"You think you are clever, don't you, Tay Ninh?" he said, his voice a harsh whisper. "You take money from the imperialists, you take money from me. For all I know you give the Americans information as well!"

His strong grasp hurt her arm, and the more she struggled to free herself, the harder Sau Ban squeezed.

"That is not true. Take the mortar. . .it is yours."

"As you can see, I already have the mortar," he sniffed, and lifted her to such an angle that only the toes of one foot touched the floor. "What do you know of Douh?"

Tay Ninh gasped at the pain in her arm and shoulder. Her words came in a rush. "He is going to a village. Please, Sau Ban. I haven't—"

"When?"

"Tonight."

"Alone?"

"No . . . with the soldiers . . . a special mission."

"What village are the Americans so interested in?"

"Xon Dao . . . the village is Xon Dao!"

The name of the village threw him. "Xon Dao," Sau Ban said. "What do they want there?"

"Douh said they need to ask a question of the villagers . . . they leave before daylight. That is all I know. Please, Sau Ban. Put me down."

Sau Ban held her in place a moment longer then flung her across the room where she slammed into the side of the bunker, and slid to the floor.

For long seconds they eyed each other. The outline of Tay Ninh's small breasts rose and fell with each quick breath, nipples grazed the silky black fabric of her blouse. Her heels scraped over the floor, until her back pressed into the wall and she could go no farther.

Sau Ban watched, his excitement grew with her fear of him. His hand moved to the erection beneath his shorts. He massaged it, never taking his eyes from hers.

Tay Ninh turned her head from the sight, choking back a wad of spit that seemed to catch in her throat.

"You are a clever bitch, aren't you, Tay Ninh?" Sau Ban cooed.

She said nothing, only watched as he slipped a hand down the loose waist band of his shorts and stepped out of them. His brown skin gleamed with the color of copper in the lamp light. His cock stood out from the deep shadows of his middle and waved from side to side like a snake stretching itself from a tree.

With a speed that startled her, he leaped to where she lay. Tay Ninh kicked at his legs and tried to scream, but Sau Ban's hand clamped over her mouth, cutting the sound off in her throat. He bent her head back and glared into her eyes.

"You once asked me what I would enjoy, Tay Ninh! Do you remember?" he whispered, and backed her into the side of the bunker.

Tay Ninh's eyes were wild above his hand, but she couldn't make a sound.

His lips fluttered against her ear. "Tonight I will show you."

With his free hand Sau Ban grabbed her hair, forcing Tay Ninh to her knees. He shoved her head into the bunker entrance, and when she struggled, he kicked her in the side hard enough to knock the wind from her.

He was on her in an instant, and shoved her to her stomach. He held her hands above her head, and jerked her pants down with the other. His fingers scratched and kneaded painfully between her legs until he'd forced them apart. He entered her with a quick powerful thrust and stopped, pinning her hips to the floor.

She felt the air being sucked from her lungs, and fought to refill them.

His fingers encircled her neck, squeezing until she thought she would pass out. When he released his grip, she lay gasping, close to unconsciousness.

"That is how it feels in your stinking tunnel!"

He began to move.

"No!" she screamed.

He shoved into her with a brutal, steady pace.

Her mouth opened as if to scream again, but his hand at her throat stopped it.

"Not yet," he gasped. "I will tell you when it is time to scream."

When her body went limp he released her neck and slammed his hips into her with such a thrust that she felt something tear. She took the air back in a long wheeze. There were small objects swarming over the bunker's walls. Her spine burned from tail to brain stem. She didn't know if her eyes were open or closed. She could no longer feel anything but the pain inside her buttocks, the rocking, ever-increasing rhythm of it.

"Feel the pressure. The way it builds in your chest. Do you? Do you feel it!" He choked, shaking her head against the hard floor for an answer.

But the words were faint in Tay Ninh's ear. She saw herself standing outside the bunker. The warm sun bright on her face. There was a pool of clear water nearby. White egrets waded in it. They jabbed at fish with their sharp beaks. In her mind's-eye she was suddenly naked and swimming with the fishes. They schooled around her, nibbling delicately at her fingers and toes with their soft lips.

His fingers continued to press into her throat with a steady pressure, his breath was moist, dog-like on her face.

"Scream!"

The clear water grew hot and thick—the fish, angry and biting. Their soft lips were replaced by tiny rasping teeth. They chewed at her arms and legs, pulling at her, drawing her farther into the growing darkness of the pool. Her hands slapped at the fish, her feet tried to kick them away.

Sau Ban had both hands on her throat now, his arms extended, his full weight pressing down on her neck.

"Scream for Sau Ban! Scream!"

Tay Ninh's mouth opened. Her lungs filled with the fetid water. She grew heavy, sinking into the swirling blackness.

Chapter 19

Luck was still running in the squad's favor. The LP they'd drawn for the night was located by the river, and just like Clayborn promised, the LP was close to the camp. Tucker took the point as the squad filed through the main gate. It would be a fairly simple matter to slip away when the time came. The cover along the river would work nicely to hide their departure.

When they reached the river, Tucker suggested to Clayborn that the squad set up to either side of the path. Tucker, Preacher, Monroe and Conroy would take one side, Clayborn, Douh, and Leon the other. Clayborn agreed, and after deciding how long each man's watch would be, the men moved into the nipa palm for the night.

Before leaving the camp, the squad, minus Clayborn, had held one last meeting, and Leon continued to do his best to find reasons for them not to go.

"I still don't like the idea of just leaving Clayborn alone like that," he said.

"I told you, Leon. We ain't leaving until just before daylight. Clayborn's gonna be close enough to the camp that he could piss into it if he wanted. Ain't nothing gonna happen. Quit worrying, will you?"

"Yeah. Even that fool could find his way back from there," Monroe chuckled.

"Well, buddy," Tucker finally said. "Are you in or out?"

Leon stared at each of their faces in turn. "I'm in, but for the record I still don't like it," he said. No one had noticed before, but Leon had taken Tucker's lucky helmet from the pole outside the hootch.

Leon saw Tucker staring at the helmet, and returned him a sheepish look. "You don't mind, do you?"

Tucker stepped forward and slapped him on the back with a

good-natured pat. "Little luck might be just the thing, Leon."

Tucker faced the rest of the men.

"All right," he said. "Preacher, you're carrying the radio. It will be on our side of the path. We'll let Clayborn have the first watch, tell him it's a Christmas present or something, after that the rest is easy. I'll take the last watch. Halfway through it, Leon, you and Doe-doe come over to our side and we'll be gone. Agreed?"

Everyone nodded except Leon.

Tucker eyed his old friend. For the first time since coming up with the idea of getting Monroe's dad an orchid, he had a twinge of misgiving. It would be all right, he reassured himself. They had a radio, and if for some reason they couldn't avoid trouble, well, they could always call for support. He knew battalion would never just leave their asses hanging out to dry. They weren't deserters. Most likely they'd be given Article-15's. And what was that? A loss of rank? They were all privates now, rank didn't mean anything. Tucker figured some day, maybe years from now, he and Leon might even look back on this and laugh.

Chapter 20

Tuan waited with the mortar tube in the exit pit for Sau Ban. Lugging the heavy piece of equipment through the tunnel had done him in. By the time he reached the pit he was exhausted. He hoped Sau Ban would take his time arriving, and he went to sleep.

If Tuan found the going difficult with the mortar tube, the five mortar rounds Sau Ban had to bring were no better. There didn't seem to be any easy way to move them along in the bulky rucksack Tay Ninh had put them in. The tunnel was too narrow for him to wear the thing on his shoulders, and like Tuan had done with the tube, Sau Ban was forced to scoot the ruck ahead, then crawl to it, repeating the process over and over again. When he came to the hole in the tunnel's ceiling, he spent a long time catching his breath, and thinking. Maybe he'd been taking the wrong approach to killing Douh? Maybe it wasn't as important to know when Douh left the camp as it was to know when he was in it? He thought of how it might be to enter the camp through the hole some night and kill him in his sleep? He thought of Tay Ninh. He chased the thought away. On his stomach again, he shoved the bag as far as he could, then pulled himself forward.

Sau Ban was in his familiar mood by the time the tunnel ended. When he found Tuan sleeping it made him angry enough to swat him on the head again.

"Stupid ass!" Sau Ban scolded in a whisper. "Someday you will sleep forever! Now get going," he said, and pushed Tuan up and out of the pit.

Once they were free of the tunnel, Sau Ban slipped his arms through the straps of the rucksack, then shouldered the mortar tube as well. The weight was more than enough for two men, but Sau Ban wanted to make good time, and knew the skinny Tuan had all he could do carrying himself and their rifles.

With Tuan keeping close in the darkness, they set off along the river.

Chapter 21

A half moon hung low to the horizon, and the river shined like a polished table-top in its reflection. Now and then Tucker could see nipa palm and reeds floating past, their silhouettes breaking the river's gloss with tiny ripples.

Tucker checked his watch, the luminous hands said 0400. Time to go. Leon lifted to a sitting position the moment Tucker whispered his name across the path. Douh was already up.

Clayborn lay to the far side of them, his back turned, his poncho wrapped tightly around him from head to foot in the early morning chill.

With Tucker walking point, the squad stuck close to the river until they reached the first western treeline. There, Tucker cut into it, heading for the open paddies on the other side.

The six men walked for a half-hour when Monroe, bringing up the rear, passed word for a halt. They weren't moving very fast anyway, because once inside the trees, Tucker was forced to go to all fours on the path, feeling with his hands for trip wires.

In short order, Monroe passed along another message and Tucker could hear safeties clicking before the words reached him.

They were being followed.

In nearly silent motion the men took staggered, prone positions to either side of the path and waited. No one moved.

Monroe cupped a hand over his ear and listened again. Whoever was following them had stopped. Palm fronds scraped together overhead, a lone frog chirped for a mate, but there was nothing else to hear. Then came the audible click of a ring striking a plastic rifle stock.

"Damn," Monroe said under his breath. He now figured he knew who it was. A moment later and Monroe could see Clayborn's dark form moving slowly toward him.

"You get yourself shot coming up like that, Lieutenant," he said in a half whisper, watching Clayborn drop to his stomach.

"Monroe. That you?"

"It's me all right. Come on in," Monroe answered, and went to a crouch. Everyone else did the same. A few moments later Clayborn knelt with them and didn't waste time getting right to the point.

"What's this all about? Where are you men going?"

There wasn't anything to do but tell him, and Tucker knew it. Besides, they were away from the camp, and it was too late for Clayborn to try and stop them now.

"We're going to a village, Lieutenant," Tucker whispered, and crawled up beside him. "Won't do no good to talk about it, because we're going."

Clayborn tried to see their faces. Tucker's was the only one he could make out well enough.

"What village? Why?"

"It ain't what you think, Lieutenant. We wanna find an orchid." In a different time, Tucker could have laughed at how that sounded.

"Orchid?"

"Not now, Lieutenant. We need to do this. That's all." Tucker pointed in the direction of the camp. "If I was you, I'd wait until it gets light before going back in."

Clayborn glanced up through the trees at the graying sky. He looked down and scanned the row of faces that he could see better now. If he was going to lose a squad of men by having them walk away, it wasn't going to be this one. Not 2nd. Not without him.

"I'm coming with you," Clayborn said.

"You don't need to do—"

"Don't tell me what I need to do, Burdick. We came out here together, and we're going back in together."

By now Monroe had moved up next to Clayborn and crouched beside him. "If the man says he's with us, it's okay by me."

A silence followed that no one filled, and finally Tucker spoke.

"All right, Lieutenant. But here's how it is. This ain't an Army operation. Out here there's no rank. This whole thing is my idea, and I'm leading it."

"Fair enough," Clayborn said without a moment's hesitation. He looked at the sky again, where the stars were beginning to fade. "Think we better get going?"

Tucker stared up to where light was coming quickly over the trees.

"No. We might as well wait a while longer. It'll be light enough for us to move through here faster in a few minutes."

Clayborn slid to the other side of the path, and like the rest, waited silently for the sunrise, his head cocked as if he might hear it coming.

Chapter 22

It was midday when the squad filed out of the last treeline and could see Xon Dao ahead of them. Its dry brown huts provided a sharp contrast to the greenery surrounding the village. Scattered throughout the paddies, women in conical straw hats worked, stooped in the tall rice plants.

"So far so good," Tucker said to no one in particular, and after a quick scan of the area, led the men to the candy-stripe that ran through Xon Dao.

Sau Ban spotted the soldiers in an instant. He and Tuan had long since arrived, and Sau Ban was now hiding in a hedgerow a short distance away from the village. Tuan was with his mother. Sau Ban had sent him into the village to learn what he could about the American's visit. It was a dangerous move. Sau Ban knew the soldiers would be suspicious of a boy Tuan's age living at home instead of being in the army. But there were questions Sau Ban wanted answers to, and sending Tuan into the village seemed the only way of getting them.

He counted the seven men now halfway to the village, easily picking out Douh's small frame among them. Everything was as Tay Ninh had said.

Now his problem was how to get Douh alone. More than anything he wanted to separate him from the soldiers. But the squad outnumbered Sau Ban three to one, and he wasn't about to take them all on at once if he could help it. Whatever else he thought of them, he could see by the way the soldiers went about their march that they were not sloppy troops. The men were well spaced on the dike, and each kept an alert watch about him.

His thoughts wandered back to the tunnel, the entrance it provided to the camp. To be inside the camp was an idea that fascinated Sau Ban the more he thought about it. It would be suicide, but how many soldiers could he kill before they killed him? And what if he survived? A one-man assault on an American base camp would be the stuff of military legend. Sau Ban pondered this last thought a good while. In the meantime, the soldiers were entering the village.

The squad received a different reception than on their earlier visit. People came out of their homes just as before, but this time the children were subdued, and none yelled for chop-chop.

"Wasn't like this the last time," Monroe said.

"Sure wasn't," Conroy said.

"Which hootch did you find the beans in, Preach?" Tucker asked.

Preacher looked first one way then the other. "They all look alike."

"It's that one down there at the end," Leon said.

Preacher and Conroy stayed outside the hut for security, and the other five men crowded into Tuan's home.

"Look on the shrine," Preacher yelled through the doorway.

Everyone did. Everyone but Monroe. He kept his eyes on Tuan, who sat at the table alone.

The box was still where Preacher remembered, and Tucker quickly opened it. The beans were there as well.

Just then there was a commotion outside and Tuan's mother hurried through the doorway. She'd been in the paddies since morning and didn't know Tuan had returned. Her first inclination upon seeing him was to rush to where he sat, but she turned her eyes to the soldiers, trying to remain calm.

"Ask her where these things came from, Doe-doe," Tucker said, holding up the box.

Douh stepped forward and bowed politely. "*The soldiers would like to know where you found these beans.*"

She only shook her head at this.

Douh tried again, pointing at the box. "*These beans. Where do the orchids grow that they come from? Tell and we will be gone.*"

Again she shook her head, but now she stared at the dirt floor.

"What's wrong, Douh?" Clayborn asked. "Why doesn't she answer?"

"I do not know."

"What about this guy?" Monroe said and everyone turned to

look at Tuan.

With the soldiers watching him, Tuan grew so nervous he began to kick the table leg. He looked at his mother, but she continued to stare at the floor.

"Ask him, Doe-doe," Tucker said.

Douh took a firm voice when he addressed Tuan. "*You have been listening. Answer our question.*"

Tuan straightened himself in the chair. He knew he had to say something. "*They come from far away.*"

"*Where?*"

"*There,*" Tuan said, waving to the west.

"What's he saying, Doe-doe?"

"He says the flowers come from far away to the west."

Tucker took the map from his leg pocket and knelt, spreading the map on the floor.

Clayborn and Leon moved in closer and looked down with him, though they both knew what lay to the west.

"Ask him if they're in the Plain of Reeds."

Douh did.

"*Yes. That's right. The Plain of Reeds.*"

"He says, yes, Tucker."

Tucker carried the map to the table and spread it there. Tuan stared down at the map.

Tucker pointed to where Xon Dao was marked on the map. "Tell him this is the village. Can he show us on the map how far the orchids are?"

Douh asked the question, and Tuan stared at him with a blank expression.

"This is maybe the first map he has seen," Douh explained.

"Great. Now what?" Leon piped up from where he stood behind them all.

Everyone glanced back at Leon, then shifted their eyes to Tucker, who pulled on his bottom lip and studied Tuan.

"Hell," Tucker muttered after a time. "Why would he need a map? He knows where the things are growing. He can show us."

"Follow him out there?" Leon nearly screamed.

"That's where he said they were, didn't he?"

The men looked at one another with fleeting glances, and Monroe got to his feet.

"For once I'm with Leon on this, Tucker. We got no business fuckin' around in there. Besides," Monroe said, jerking his thumb at Tuan. "This guy is so nervous I'm starting to fidget with him. If he ain't Charlie Cong, then I don't know who is."

Everyone stared at Tuan, who returned a weak smile.

Monroe leaned over the tabled and his eyes bored into Tuan's. "You VC?"

Tuan's face dropped its smile, and he shook his head violently. "No VC."

"Ask him what he's doing here, Doe-doe," Monroe said without taking his eyes off Tuan. "Why's he just hangin' round the shack?"

Douh took a place at the table. "*The soldiers want to know why you are not an ARVN.*"

Before Tuan had a chance to answer, his mother pushed through the men and stood next to him at the table.

"*My only child,*" she said, addressing Douh. "*The ARVN say they will take him soon. He is a good boy who would never run with the Viet Cong.*"

"Mamasan's got a voice after all," Monroe said.

Douh turned to Tucker. "She claims he is not yet old enough for the ARVN."

Monroe snorted in disgust. "Maybe not for them." He leaned over the table once more and took one of Tuan's hands, turning it palm up. The skin had been rubbed raw from the crawl in the tunnel. Monroe stood him up and looked at his knees. The skin there was much the same.

"You fall down?" Monroe asked.

Douh translated, and Tuan stared down at his knees like he wanted to see what the soldiers were looking at. He thought quickly.

"*Yesterday a water buffalo bucked after seeing a snake. I fell.*"

"*You should be more careful,*" Douh said.

"*That old buffalo has had it in for me since I can remember.*" Tuan smiled, doing his best to sound like he were among friends.

"He says it is from falling off a buffalo."

"Or crawling around in places he don't belong," Monroe said.

At that moment, Preacher screamed in the doorway. "I think we got some movement out here!"

"Keep an eye on him, Leon," Tucker said as the men hurried for the door.

Outside, Preacher was pointing in the direction of the hedgerow. "I could swear I seen somebody moving on the other side of that thing."

Everyone looked, but there was nothing to see.

"We better take a look," Preacher said.

Tucker put a hand on his arm. "We didn't come here for that. There's a cease-fire, remember. If we make contact out here it'll be worse for us when we get back."

"I don't like this place," Monroe said after a time. "The natives are restless, my man. Something ain't right."

"You're telling me," Preacher said. "They're all staring at us like they're waiting for something to happen. You know what I mean?"

Tucker glanced at the villagers standing silently outside their homes. "Di di mau. Go. Di di," he yelled, and waved his arms in a shooing manner.

Like they thought there wasn't a second to lose, people began crowding back into their homes. One little boy stayed where he was, staring at the men until his mother ran out and pulled him into the house.

"They weren't afraid the last time," Preacher said.

Monroe stared down the length of the village. "What now, Tucker?"

"I don't know," he answered, still watching the hedgerow. He reached inside his shirt and touched the tattoo, then examined the pus it left on his fingertip. "If those orchids are close enough I'd still like to go for 'em."

"The kid says they're a long ways away," Monroe reminded him.

Tucker peeked over his shoulder, then back to the hedgerow. "You saw the way he looked at the map. What's long for him might not be long for us."

"It's a bad place," Monroe said as if Tucker needed to be reminded.

"It'd be a shame to go back now," Tucker murmured, then turned to Clayborn. "What do you think, Lieutenant?

Clayborn couldn't produce a thought, let alone give an answer. He hadn't expected Tucker to ask for his opinion.

"I can go with whatever the squad decides," he said. He'd never been closer to the men, and he enjoyed the camaraderie. He was one of them now. No rank. No one looking to him for direction or leadership. And for the first time in his life he felt like a soldier. In truth, Clayborn didn't want the men to go back without getting what they had come for.

"If my vote's worth anything, I say we go for it," Clayborn finally added.

"Preach? What about you an' Conroy?" Tucker asked.

"Yeah. Long as it ain't too far. I'd like to be back in time for Christmas," Preacher answered.

Conroy peeked at Monroe, who scowled and said nothing.

"I'll go," Conroy squeaked.

Monroe looked at all their faces in turn. "Looks like we're gonna see this thing through, then. But like Preach says, I don't wanna spend my Christmas in that bad ass place."

"Bring that guy out here, Leon," Tucker called.

In a second they were both outside with the squad gathered around them. Preacher continued to watch the hedgerow.

"This guy is going to lead us to the flowers," Tucker said, addressing Douh and Leon. Tucker raised his hand before Leon could protest. "We already voted, Leon. Everybody's in."

"Damn it all, Tuck! We're gonna be out here for a week!"

Tucker held his rifle over one shoulder, his hand gripping the barrel. "Doe-doe. Ask him if we can get there before dark."

Douh did the translation.

"He says, if you were to go now, maybe."

"We can be home sometime Christmas day," Tucker said.

"Shit on a stick," Leon said, kicked his boot in the dirt and walked off.

Tucker had Douh inform Tuan of what the plans were. Hearing that her son was being taken away by the American soldiers sent his mother into a fit of wailing that lasted until Douh convinced her it would be all right. Before the squad left, she rushed into her house then back out with a coconut, shoving it into Tuan's hands, and patting his cheek.

"She'll probably do the same thing when we're gone and he turns back into Luke The Gook," Monroe said, adding: "If this guy ain't a dink, my ass is white."

Tucker ignored Monroe, and motioned them all forward. And one by one the men fell in line, following Tuan out of the village and into the Plain of Reeds.

Sau Ban watched the soldiers move away, waiting until they were out of sight before he could relax enough to think clearly. This new turn of events concerned him. The Americans were behaving strangely. He knew by the way Tuan was allowed to walk freely that they hadn't taken him prisoner, and Sau Ban couldn't understand why they were taking him in the first place. He finally decided there was only one way to find out, and after making sure the soldiers were not doubling back, Sau Ban entered the village to ask.

When Sau Ban stepped in the doorway, Tuan's mother was sitting at the table, crying and clutching the small wooden box.

Upon seeing him, she rushed from the table and began blabbering about how the long noses were going to kill Tuan.

Sau Ban stared at the box she waved under his nose.

"The long noses will kill him!" she screamed in his face.

"Silence!" he snapped.

"My son!"

"Silence!" he ordered again, but she continued ranting.

"He is a good boy! You know this! Save him from the devils!"

To quiet her, Sau Ban drew his hand back in a threatening manner. He snatched the box from her hands and looked inside. He recognized the contents, but the beans meant nothing and he threw the box across the room.

This set her to wailing until Sau Ban slapped her face and her voice dropped to a soft whimper.

"My son is dead."

Sau Ban took her by the arm and shoved her roughly into a chair at the table.

"Why have the soldiers taken Tuan? Where is he leading them?" he barked, hovering over her.

She pointed to where the beans lay on the floor. "They want to find the flowers."

"What?"

"The soldiers want to know where the flowers are," she said, and her voice broke into sobs once more.

"He is leading them to the forest?"

She only nodded, and Sau Ban paced around the room, stopping to stare down at the beans.

"Why do the Americans want the flowers?"

She shook her head. "They did not say. Please, Sau Ban. They will kill him. I know."

If they don't I will, he thought, but didn't say as much. His mind was occupied with other matters. Through blind luck the soldiers had managed to stumble on Tuan and the fool was going to lead them to the Dinh Ba.

"What did he tell them about the forest?" he demanded.

For the first time it dawned on her that she possibly had more to fear from Sau Ban than she did the American soldiers, and she eyed him suspiciously. "He told them nothing, Sau Ban."

He began pacing once more. Perhaps this wasn't so bad. Three of his men were already in the forest. He knew the forest, knew there was only one place where the flowers could be found. Tuan guiding the Americans to the forest, stupid though it was, couldn't be better. In fact it was perfect. But time was of the essence. He needed to get moving.

Without another word to Tuan's mother, Sau Ban hurried out the doorway and back to the hedgerow. He hid the mortar tube and rucksack, knowing the villagers would not come near his things. He wished he could carry the mortar and rounds along, but the added weight would slow him too much.

He slung both his and Tuan's rifles over one shoulder, and broke into a jog for the first treeline heading southwest for the Dinh Ba Forest.

Chapter 23

The men saw the forest from a ways off: they couldn't miss it. The forest appeared to be an island floating in undulating, tall elephant grass. There wasn't another tree for at least a thousand meters.

A good rain was falling by the time the squad finished pushing blindly through the high grass and reached the edge of the forest. The rain looked like it planned to stay a while. The men moved into the trees and set up a circular, night defensive perimeter. Clayborn had been the only one to bring his rucksack, and in it, something even Tucker in his careful planning had neglected to think of bringing: an entrenching tool. Each of the men took turns using the shovel to dig shallow foxholes in the soft dirt.

Twilight was fast upon them. The rain let up, leaving a damp fog to hover the ground in the eerie calm of the forest. The men huddled in their foxholes. The smokers cupped their hands over the day's last cigarette. Soon most everyone had settled in for the night.

By 1900, Leon lay on his back, sleeping, the poncho pulled to his neck. Tucker's helmet covered his face, its holes providing good ventilation.

Tuan had been allowed to hollow out a place for himself, then, at Monroe's insistence, his hands were tied behind his back as a precaution. He lay on his side in the hole, silently blowing away the mosquitoes attacking his face.

Conroy had fallen asleep the minute his eyes closed, and Preacher wasn't far behind.

Monroe had scooted over to Tucker's foxhole and lay beside him, whispering.

"Be straight with me, Tucker. How much trouble you think we're in when we get back?"

Tucker shrugged under his poncho. "Kinda late for that, ain't it?"

"Maybe."

"The way I figure it, Top will try and have us busted. So what? We lose some pay."

"What if Leon's right? What if they say we're deserters? They put guys in the Long Binh Jail for that."

"Deserters don't go back. Remember that guy who took off right after we got in-country? What's his name. . .Slater, yeah, now he's a deserter. The MP's been looking for him in Saigon for over nine months. Us? Tomorrow morning we'll only have been gone twenty-four hours. You know how Top is. It'll blow over in a few days."

Monroe murmured something that Tucker couldn't hear.

"We'll be in and out first thing in the morning," Tucker whispered back. "You saw the size of it. This place can't be more than sixty acres or so at the most. Week from now, an orchid will be sitting at your dad's place back in the world, and we will have done what we said we were gonna do."

Monroe didn't have anything more to add, so he made a move to crawl back to his foxhole, but paused, hanging his face close to Tucker's, leaving him with a last thought. "Like it or not, Clayborn's gonna take the heat for this," he whispered.

Tucker said nothing, and in another moment, Monroe vanished into the darkness and the perimeter grew quiet once more.

Mosquitoes buzzed ears and faces. Crickets and cicadas hummed in separate rhythms from inside the forest. And the frogs, the frogs were always there. The air was thick. Damp. The smell of rotting vegetation everywhere.

The squad had voted for two, one-hour watches, and Clayborn drew the first hour. He listened to the sporadic, soft rustle of ponchos and bodies around him, and forced his thoughts to something other than that night on the canal. His eyes might just as well been closed. For a time he distracted himself by closing his eyes, then opening them to see if there really was a difference. He couldn't decide. Gradually his mind drifted to the letter he'd mailed to Sheila. Clayborn could only guess at her reaction once she learned of his decision to leave the service. Most likely it meant the end of his marriage. He spent a good while considering the possibility, wondering if it really mattered anymore. And why should it? Would anything ever be important to him again? So far there wasn't anything in his life that had counted for much. He would be the first to admit he'd never been good at anything. Clayborn guessed his existence so far was about as invisible as a life could get. Now this. A war. And like everything in the years preceding it, he had somehow managed to fade into its background.

The hypnotic sounds of the forest pulsed around him, the darkness covered him like a shroud. He felt invisible. A man occupying space, disembodied, slowly becoming a part of it all.

At daybreak, the rain started again, but none of the men seemed to notice: they were already so cold and wet it no longer counted for much. Everyone hunched silently over balls of burning C4, heating their canned breakfasts in the chill dawn light.

Monroe untied Tuan's hands, and lent him his bayonet so he could crack open his coconut.

"Ask him where the orchids are from here, Doe-doe," Tucker said, and shoved a last spoonful of shredded beef in his mouth, watching Tuan work the bayonet into the hard coconut meat.

Douh and Tuan exchanged words. "He says they are farther back in the forest."

Tucker wiped his mouth on a sleeve and stood, checking the time. "We best get going," he said.

The operation was taking longer than he'd promised. Even if the orchids were in their hands this very minute, the squad had a hard day of humping back to camp and everyone knew it. The men were still in fairly good spirits, but Tucker knew this could change in a heartbeat if they ended up spending another miserable wet night in the field when they didn't have to.

They finished their meals in a hurry. The men rolled and laced their ponchos to back of their web belts. They stuffed the rest of their C-rations back inside o.d. socks and tied them across their backs with boot laces. In short order the squad was ready to move out.

The men fell into the same column as the day before. Douh walked behind Tuan, Tucker and the rest following. With each meter the new-growth nipa palm thickened until their speed was reduced to a crawl.

Chapter 24

Sau Ban busied himself at the ambush site as the squad made its way through the forest. If Tuan's mother had spoken the truth, then there was only one place the soldiers were heading. The flowers they were after grew in the trees surrounding an elongated opening in the forest. And Sau Ban's position was to the far tip of the clearing, the rest of his men were strung out in the trees off to one side. After the soldiers entered the kill zone, his men were to hold their fire until Sau Ban had a chance to take out the radioman, more importantly, the radio itself. Sau Ban wanted the soldiers on his terms. Let them learn what it was to fight for their lives without the luxury of calling for air strikes and artillery. He would show them what kind of troops they were. A valuable lesson, he thought, but one none of them would live to learn from. Douh, of course, was to be spared. With the radio gone, there would be little need to hurry the killing. Sau Ban and his men could pick and choose. It would be like shooting cattle in a pen. When all had been killed, he'd have his men drag their carcasses to the edge of the forest and line them up so they could be seen from the air. He'd hang Douh from a tree above them.

The hardest part was the waiting. The rain covered all sound, muffled the air, and Sau Ban couldn't hear the soldier's approach. But then he caught the flickering motion of movement through the openings in the trees. The soldiers were coming. Sau Ban thumbed off his rifle's safety, snugging the butt firmly into his shoulder.

Once the squad broke through the nipa palm the walking became easier. The forest was still thick, but at least the men could now see where they were going.

Like water pouring from a thousand spouts, rain streamed from the palm fronds overhead and fell to the spongy floor of the forest. The dank air was overpowering.

Monroe pushed forward until he stopped beside Tucker. He pulled the towel from around his neck and mopped his head.

"I don't remember it ever being this hot. You?" he said, and unscrewed the cap from one of his canteens. He then drank a careful measure of water.

"No," Tucker answered, and joined him in a drink. "But it can't be much farther. The place isn't that big."

Without being asked, Douh put the question to Tuan, then turned to Tucker and Monroe with a smile. "You are correct, Tucker. He says we are almost there."

Monroe hooked his canteen back to his web belt and watched Tuan, who bobbed his head, trying to see past the trees. In reflex, Monroe drew the rifle under one arm, his hand squeezing and relaxing on the weapon's pistol grip.

"Answer me something, my man."

"What's that?" Tucker murmured.

"How come that little prick know about this place, anyway?"

"I been wondering the same thing," Clayborn said, and drew up a short distance away. "Who brought him here in the first place?"

Tuan glanced at the three of them, then quickly back to the forest.

"Doe-doe."

"Yes, Tucker?"

"Tell him that if anything happens, Monroe here is going to shoot him." Then to Monroe and Clayborn: "That'll give him something to think about."

Douh translated and Tuan's eyes shifted nervously from Douh to the men and back, but he said nothing in return.

Tucker pulled the map from his leg pocket. Near as I can figure this is where we are," he said, and pointed at the grid marks on the map. "Preach. You better check out that radio, just in case."

Preacher bent low so Leon could turn the radio on for him. Squelch broke over the handset.

"Bravo Charlie, this is Charlie one six. Do you copy? Over."

In another moment a voice spoke loud enough for everyone to hear. "Charlie one six, this is Bravo Charlie. Read you loud and clear, over."

"Good enough," Tucker said. "Turn it off before they start asking questions."

Tucker peered ahead at the thinning trees. "All right. Let's get this over with and go home."

The squad covered the last few meters in minutes, and soon stood at the edge of the clearing.

"*I found the beans here*," Tuan said.

"We are here, Tucker," Douh announced.

Monroe crouched next to a tree and ran his gaze over the clearing. Waist-high ferns covered the ground. Except for the constant dribble of rain falling, the clearing was quiet. Nothing seemed out of place.

"The rest of you stay put," Tucker said. "Come on, Monroe. Let's have a look."

The two of them plodded cautiously into the center of the clearing. Tucker kept a lookout while Monroe did a slow circle and studied the trees. One looked the same as the other.

"I was afraid a this," Monroe said in a hushed tone.

"What?"

"They ain't in bloom. We're gonna have to look for their vines."

Tucker waved in the rest of the squad.

Leon meandered off to one side, gawking from one tree to the next. "So where's the orchids, Tuck?"

"They're here. Monroe says we gotta find their vines, is all. We'll dig one up and be on our way."

"How are we supposed to know what to look for?" Leon whined in disgust. "There's gotta be a hundred trees around this thing."

"Ask him if he knows what trees they grow on, Doe-doe," Tucker said.

After a brief discussion with Tuan, Douh pointed toward the far end. "He remembers them as being down there."

"Okay," Tucker said. "Everybody spread out and start looking."

"And what if he's full of shit?" said Leon.

"Then I guess we're fucked, ain't we, buddy," he snapped. "You don't wanna help? Fine. Stay here and keep an eye on this guy. But quit your goddamn whining, will you? It's too late for that now."

Leon and Tucker's eyes locked while they shared a strained silence, then Leon turned his back, and said nothing.

The men were spread out and moving across the clearing when

Sau Ban opened the ambush with a three-round burst.

Preacher began to dance like he'd suddenly stepped barefoot on hot coals. The force of the bullets slamming into the radio lifted his back in an arch, spun him in a half circle. Chunks of radio sprayed the air. AK-47s cracked. Tracers ripped through the clearing in flashes of green, and the men dove for cover, now pressing themselves into the ground, heads covered in first-reflex. Ferns shredded only inches above them. Pieces blew into their faces, stinging them like angry bees. For one horrible pulse the world narrowed to a blinding white hot point of light, then just as quickly exploded into fragments of color.

Each man was now lying in the thick ferns. None could see the other. None could see exactly where the enemy was. Tucker was the first to return fire. In a mindless reaction he emptied his rifle in a two-second burst, tore out the clip, and shoved another one home. He didn't have a target, only sound at which to aim.

Monroe, only a few feet away, burrowed into the ground, smothered his face in the dirt, raised his weapon and fired off a clip without looking.

By now, Clayborn too was fighting back. The M-16 rattled in his hands, then stopped. His fingers fumbled to eject the empty clip. When he finally succeeded, in his panic, he shoved the same clip back in and pulled the trigger on an empty chamber. Thinking his weapon jammed, he rolled to his back and snatched a grenade from his belt. After two tries he managed to pull the pin, but his fingers were wrapped so tightly around the grenade, that the first time he went to throw the thing, it stayed in his hand. He tried again, this time launching it in a high arc above the ferns at the same time his arm slapped down like it had been struck with a baseball bat. Clayborn stared at the spot where a second before his thumb had been. Surprisingly there was little blood, and even less pain. When the grenade exploded the firing from the trees halted, then renewed its intensity.

Douh couldn't pry his eyes open, or pull his head from beneath his folded arms. He knew he should do something, but was afraid to draw fire on his position. Behind him he could hear a man scream for his mother, and he tried to focus on the sound, on who it might be.

It was Leon who was the farthest away from the fighting. He

and Tuan had fallen only a foot apart when the ambush began. Leon hadn't fired a shot yet. His rifle had landed beneath him, and he tugged at it while trying not to move.

The firing from the trees became sporadic. Sau Ban's men were conserving ammo, no longer shooting wildly into the foliage, they were now looking for specific targets.

Leon could hear voices, words he didn't understand. At first he thought it was Tuan trying to speak to him, then realized the words were coming from farther away. With the muddled clarity of a person waking from a long sleep, Leon realized it was the enemy. They were talking to each other, making human sounds. This wasn't some mindless beast feeding itself on the squad. It had a face, a face like the one he was staring at. Tuan's face. And it could be killed, made to stop.

"Make it stop!" Leon screamed.

With a deft movement Leon rolled to his side and grabbed his weapon, then pressed the barrel into Tuan's face.

"I said, Make it stop!"

Ferns shredded suddenly beside his face and Leon pulled the trigger without thinking. The top of Tuan's head blew away, splattering the greenery behind him with pink froth. Leon stared at the colors, looking, but not seeing what was left of Tuan's face.

"It's okay now," he said. "It's going to stop."

Leon's thoughts took a strange turn. He felt light-headed, elevated. He was suddenly on his feet. The trees sparkled with orange flashes. Green tracers came and went like cornfield fireflies on an August night. Several buzzed near his ear and he shook his face at the annoyance. He felt something slap the helmet from his head. Tears blurred his vision. He emptied his weapon on a dead run and reloaded just as quickly. His movements were automatic, precise.

On the other end of the clearing, Tucker and Monroe went to their feet with him, charging from the other side. Monroe threw a grenade. A moment later the explosion blew a black-clad body in the air.

Leon swept his barrel back and forth, spraying the area in front of him. He could see two men crawling through the nipa palm. He fired into their backs, shoved in another clip and emptied it once more. Monroe and Tucker joined him. Like sharks in a feeding frenzy, they squeezed off rounds into the bodies at their feet.

The soldiers on the other side of the clearing were beyond reason, and so was Sau Ban. His rifle had jammed after shooting the radio, and he'd been forced to watch helplessly while the ambush disintegrated before his eyes. He realized he'd been a fool not to kill Douh when he had the chance, and the thought was driving him close to rage. There was one last chance, and he knew he needed to act quickly. Sau Ban locked the long slender bayonet in place at the end of the AK's barrel and inched quietly through the ferns.

All the firing had stopped, now the only sound was that of Tucker and Monroe screaming like a pair of banshees.

Douh heard movement to his left and looked up at the very instant Sau Ban lunged the last few feet through the ferns for him.

The bayonet grazed Douh's arm, tore his shirt, and for a split second Douh felt caught up in the second act of a terrifying dream. He was staring into the crazed, wild-eyed face of Sau Ban. Douh kicked himself away from Sau Ban's next thrust. The bayonet slashed the air around him. Douh wanted to run but couldn't force himself to his feet.

Sau Ban threw the rifle like a spear. The bayonet slid easily into the wet ground between Douh's kicking legs and stayed there. A heartbeat later, and Sau Ban vanished back into the forest as quickly as he had appeared.

An eerie calm entered the clearing then. Rain dripped softly to the forest floor. A layer of blue smoke floated above the ferns.

When they recovered their senses, Tucker and Monroe rushed back to the moans of the men behind them.

Conroy had lost a lot of blood, one side of his shirt was filled with it. He complained once of being cold. His body began to tremble.

"He's going into shock!" Monroe yelled, ripped Conroy's shirt open, and stared at the ragged hole in his shoulder. "Get his feet up!"

Monroe snatched the field bandage from the band on Conroy's helmet, tore it open with his teeth then pressed it to the spot where most of the blood was coming from.

Just as quickly, Tucker grabbed the helmet, balancing Conroy's feet on it, then spun on his knees to see about Preacher.

In seconds he had Preacher's arms free of the radio and rolled him onto his stomach. The back of his shirt was blood-soaked. Here and there jagged shards of shattered radio poked from between his shoulder blades. But he hadn't been shot anywhere that Tucker could see, and he turned his attention to Clayborn, who was sitting up a few feet away, his hand held away from him at arms length while he stared at it.

Tucker reached for Clayborn's field bandage. He tied the large gauze pad over the blank part of Clayborn's hand.

"Keep your hand up if you can, Lieutenant."

"Who else is hurt?" Clayborn asked as calmly as if he wanted to know the time of day.

Tucker looked across the clearing. "Conroy and Preach," he answered, then got to his feet and headed to where Leon stood staring down at the bodies strewn around him. On the way, Tucker kicked Leon's helmet, and stopped long enough to grab it.

Leon couldn't seem to drag his eyes from the dead Viet Cong. He couldn't feel his body. Around him people were moving and speaking, but he understood nothing. Every sound came as if from a great distance. He didn't know anyone had moved next to him until Tucker touched his arm.

"Leon. You ain't hurt are you?"

Leon lifted his face to gawk at Tucker. His eyes looked like he'd only just woken.

"I don't know," Leon said, spreading his arms and staring down at himself. "I can't feel nothing."

Tucker was so happy to see Leon alive and unhurt that he had to fight off the urge to throw his arms around him. When Leon had run forward, the three VC immediately turned on him and Tucker had expected Leon to be cut down instantly. He honestly couldn't believe he wasn't. But Leon's charge had saved the squad, of that there was no doubt.

Tucker lifted the helmet back to Leon's head, gently settling it in place.

"Can you help us? Conroy's in pretty bad shape."

Leon nodded vacantly. "I'm really all right," he murmured. "They didn't kill me."

When Leon turned to face him, Tucker's head jerked at the sight. There were now four holes in the helmet forming an abstract diamond shape, and Tucker couldn't help but stare.

Leon noticed the look on his face. "What is it, Tuck?"

Tucker gazed into Leon's tired eyes. They were more green and alive at that moment than Tucker could ever recall seeing them.

"Nothing, old buddy," he said, staring at the holes once more. "Don't take that thing off your head until we get home, Leon."

There wasn't time to say more. Tucker and Leon hurried back to where Monroe was hunched over Conroy, then, suddenly remembering Douh, Tucker looked around the area.

"Doe-doe!"

With a rustle of ferns, Douh's frightened face popped up a few meters away.

"You hit?"

Douh could only shake his head. He was too embarrassed to stand up and join the others. He wanted time to clean up after soiling himself during Sau Ban's attack.

"You stay there and keep an eye out," Tucker ordered, then slid to his knees next to Monroe.

"How's he doing?"

"Ain't sure. The bleeding's stopped, but he keeps fading out on me."

Conroy's face was a pasty gray, and his eyes were closed. Monroe shook him by the chin. "Keep them eyes open, Conroy!"

Conroy's eyes fluttered open for a second, then shut once more.

"Let's see if we can move him to his side a little." Tucker said, and placed Conroy's limp right arm across his body.

With Monroe's help, they lifted Conroy's shoulder far enough from the ground for Tucker to have a look below it.

The AK round had done less damage than it could have. After passing through the radio, it didn't have enough velocity to exit Conroy's back, and there was a bruised lump the size of a baseball just below his shoulder blade.

"It didn't come out," Tucker announced.

"You hear that, Conroy? Ain't so bad, my man," Monroe said.

Conroy groaned.

"Get his feet up further, Tucker. Let's get what blood he does have back to his head."

"I'll do it," Clayborn said. He crawled toward them on his one good hand.

Tucker helped situate Conroy's feet on Clayborn's lap, then turned his attention to Preacher.

"Leon. Help me get Preach's shirt off."

Carefully they stripped the shirt from Preacher's back for a look. There were three large rips in the skin, each about two inches long and an inch deep.

"How bad is it?" Preacher grunted through the pain of being moved.

"You're torn up back here," Tucker said. "But you ain't bleeding anymore."

Tucker got to his feet and moved a short distance from the men to clear his thoughts. Their situation was about as bad as it could get, and there was no denying where the blame lay. But there wasn't time for that now. With the radio gone there could be only one way of returning to Tan Tru. Clayborn and Preacher could walk if they had to. That left Conroy, who they would have to carry. But how? They couldn't carry him on their backs, and even if they could, there was simply too much distance between them and the base camp. Suddenly, Tucker flashed on something he'd once read.

Tucker hurried over to Clayborn's rucksack and found the entrenching tool, and with Leon's help, located a pair of saplings. With the shovel, they managed to chop down the saplings in a few minutes, stripping them of their small branches until they had two sturdy poles.

"Take off your shirt, Leon," Tucker said, unbuttoning his own.

"Now button it up again," Tucker directed him.

When Leon finished, Tucker took both shirts and lay them out flat, tails facing each other. He fed one of the poles down a sleeve, up through the tail of the other shirt, and into its sleeve. Leon performed the same maneuver with the other sleeves.

Tucker checked the time. 0930. There wasn't any way they could make it back to the camp before dark, but they couldn't spend another night out here, either. They had to at least get out of the Plain of Reeds before nightfall.

Leon and Tucker carried the makeshift litter to where Monroe tended to Conroy. Having his feet elevated had helped. Conroy was at least conscious, if only half alert.

"All right. Everybody, listen up," Tucker said. "We're gonna square our shit away and get out of here. Conroy will ride on the stretcher.

The four of us," he said, indicating Douh, Leon, and Monroe, "will spell each other carrying him. Preach, you an the Lieutenant are gonna have to hump like the rest of us. Can you do it?"

Preacher, with Leon's help, had managed to right himself to a sitting position. "I think so, Tucker. I'll crawl if I have to."

"My feet are okay," Clayborn said. "I can make it."

"Good. Let's get saddled then."

It took a while to slide Conroy onto the litter, and the pain of being moved caused him to pass out once more. The stretcher fit him about as well as could be expected. His legs stuck a few inches over the end of one shirt, but his torso was supported. It would have to do.

Monroe and Tucker were crouched at either end of the poles, when Douh, who had by now cleaned himself and was standing a short distance away, pointed across the clearing.

"Look there!"

Halfway up the side of a tree, a single white orchid dangled from a small branch. The edges of its three petals were etched in brilliant orange. From where the squad stood, the flower appeared to be the size of a man's hand.

"Look. There's another one." Leon nearly screamed, pointing farther up the tree.

"So that little bastard was right after all," Monroe said.

"I'm gonna get it," Leon said, starting for the tree.

"There ain't time."

Everyone who could stopped and stared at Tucker.

"It don't mean nothing anymore. We gotta get the hell out of here. We got wounded," he said.

Monroe took a step forward. "And them things is the reason, my man."

"Where's the entrenching tool?" Leon asked.

Tucker rubbed his face with both hands in a frustrated motion, then shook Clayborn's ruck from his shoulders. "Here," he said, and tossed the shovel to Leon. "But be quick about it."

"Come on, Monroe. Show me what to look for," Leon said.

They located a tangle of vines at the base of the trunk, and Leon started digging.

"Easy does it, Leon," Monroe cautioned him. "Get as many of the roots as you can."

While Leon worked, Monroe unlaced his poncho from the back of his web belt and spread it on the ground, then motioned to Douh.

"Hey, Doe-doe. Think you can shinny up there and get one a them flowers?"

Douh handed his weapon to Monroe, happy at last to be of some help, he pulled off his boots, then went up the tree like a monkey. In another minute he plucked the orchid and dropped it down to Monroe's waiting hands.

Leon finally wedged loose a shovel-sized clump of hair-fine roots. Tucker held the vines steady while Leon made a clean cut with the shovel blade. They wrapped everything up in the poncho and looked at Monroe to see if what they'd done was okay.

But Monroe hadn't been paying attention. He was too busy examining the orchid.

The petals of the flower were thin, and their orange edges were formed into skirt-like ruffles. The orchid looked so fragile that Tucker was afraid to touch it.

"So that's what they look like," Tucker said.

That's when Monroe started to laugh: a small chuckle from deep inside his chest that soon turned into a full-blown hoot. "Oh, yeah, my man," he said, closing his eyes and shaking his head. "This what an orchid looks like all right."

"What's so funny then?" Leon asked.

Monroe grinned at them from beneath his helmet, the cleft of his chin edged in deep shadow.

"You fools don't know, do you?"

"Know what?" they said in unison.

"It ain't the kind that grows vanilla. They might be here, but this son of a bitch ain't one of them. Can you believe that shit? We been fucked after all," he said.

Wanting to salvage something from the situation, Leon asked: "Maybe it's rare?"

At this, Monroe snorted through his nose in disgust. "This goddamn thing is as common as crabs on a whore, Leon."

Clayborn called to them. "Conroy's asking for water."

The brief respite was over. All their thoughts returned to the matters at hand.

"There isn't time to look anymore," Tucker said. "We got a lot of ground to cover before nightfall."

Monroe and Tucker took their places once more on the poles of the litter. On the count of three, they lifted it from the ground.

"You ready, Monroe?" Tucker said over his shoulder.

Monroe nodded.

Tucker faced forward to where Leon waited at the head of the column.

"All right. Let's go home."

Chapter 25

Sau Ban made his escape from the forest before the Americans had the chance to hunt him down. For the first time in memory he was unsure of himself. The soldiers had fought better than he'd counted on. They had met him on his own terms, and defeated him. For that he admired them. Now he needed time to think.

Sau Ban bulled his way through the wet grass, stopping now and then to listen before pushing on. By the time he reached the safety of the trees, the air burned in his lungs. His legs, chest and arms were raw from being scraped by the coarse grass.

The first order of business was to re-arm himself. For that he would need to get back to Xon Dao. His pistol was there with the mortar tube. The handgun was of little use except at close range: the mortar just the opposite. But either one was better than nothing. Sau Ban only wanted Douh dead. How it happened was no longer so important. He was sure the Americans would come back through Xon Dao, and for a while he tried thinking of a plan, but nothing came to mind. Despite his scheming, he had missed three chances to kill the traitor. Douh seemed to be living a charmed life. Sau Ban decided that from here on he would leave it to happenstance. If he could reach the village ahead of the soldiers, maybe a new opportunity would present itself.

Sau Ban took a last look at the forest before leaving. The Americans hadn't come out of it yet. How many of them his men had killed or wounded, he had no idea. But he knew by the sound of their screams during the ambush the soldiers hadn't come through unscathed. And if they were transporting dead or wounded with them, their progress would be slowed. If nothing else, time, at least, was again on his side.

Chapter 26

It took the squad an hour to break out of the green-fisted heat of the elephant grass. Tucker's and Monroe's feet kept tangling in the grass, and more than once they came close to dropping Conroy. Now both of them were exhausted to the point of collapse.

Preacher's wounds were bleeding again, not seriously, but enough to cause some concern. Between the seven of them they had only one field bandage left. Preacher and Clayborn both insisted it be saved for Conroy. The squad was shot up, tired and hungry, but they were all still alive and heading for the safety of Tan Tru.

Monroe stayed by Conroy when the squad broke for chow. Everyone else spread out and took inventory of what rations they had left. At best they had enough for two meals per man. In the interest of time they decided to eat everything now to lighten their loads. Once they reached Xon Dao they could fill up on rice if they had to.

Tucker had just finished a meal of chicken loaf, ham and lima beans, three C-ration cookies, and fruit cake, when Douh sidled up beside him and sat down.

"You got any smokes left, Doe-doe? I lost mine somewhere."

Douh drew a plastic cigarette case from his helmet band and handed it to him, waiting until Tucker had a smoke going.

"There is something I must tell you, Tucker."

"What's that?" Tucker said, and looked up at the thinning clouds. The rain had stopped, and now it appeared as if the sun would soon be shining. If it weren't hot enough already, Tucker knew it was about to get worse.

"I saw someone in the forest who I know."

The words didn't make any sense and Tucker eyed him suspiciously.

"Say again."

Douh cleared his throat. "In the forest. A man tried to kill me while you were breaking the ambush. He came at me with a bayonet. I know him."

"How?"

"We came to the South together."

"And he came at you with a bayonet?"

"Yes. It was him."

"Things happened pretty fast back there. Guy gets to seeing—"

"No, Tucker. It was him. I have seen him before. Recently."

"Yeah, when?"

Douh stopped to clear his throat once more. "Outside the camp. By the river. He was standing in the nipa palm while we waited for the boats one evening."

"Why didn't you say something before?"

"I was too frightened. It was getting dark. The boat was coming. He ran away before I could think."

Tucker pulled at his lips with one hand. Douh's information, though curious, certainly didn't change anything as far as he could see.

"Gook's a gook, Doe-doe," he shrugged. For a moment, he wished he'd chosen his words more carefully.

"No," Douh said again. "This gook is different."

Tucker had to fight off a grin. "How so?"

"I do not believe he was in the forest by. . .I cannot think of the word. . ."

"Coincidence?"

"Yes. That is it. He was not there by coincidence."

Tucker flipped the cigarette away, gazed toward the forest, then back to Douh. "Everybody's spooked, Doe-doe. If you saw some one you recognized, then it was all chance."

"You do not know this man. When I chieu hoi, I turned him and the others in. I told the MP's where they were staying. But he escaped capture. I know he then came into the Mekong. Somehow he has learned where I am. Our country is small, yes, but I have seen him twice now. I do not believe in such chances. Sau Ban is hunting me."

Tucker couldn't believe what he was hearing. "Then the ambush—"

"Yes. Somehow Sau Ban learned where we were going. I am

sure of it. He is crazy, Tucker. All of the men were afraid of him. There is nothing he will not do."

"Then why didn't this Sau Ban shoot you when he had the chance?"

"I think he would like to take me alive."

"If what you say is true, we fucked up his plans pretty good back there. You think he'll try again?"

Douh looked back to the forest. When he finally faced Tucker once more, the corners of his lips were set deep in his round cheeks.

"He will keep trying, Tucker."

"Okay, Doe-doe," Tucker said, then reached over and squeezed Douh's arm. "Let's keep this between you and me. We got enough to worry about as it is. It's not like there ain't people trying to kill the lot of us. You see anything, you let somebody know."

Ten minutes later the men were finished eating, and Tucker issued the order of march. Leon and Douh would take the next turn at carrying Conroy. Monroe was given the drag position behind Preacher. Tucker took point, and Clayborn was to stay behind him. When they were ready to set off, Tucker offered a final instruction.

"We can't be half-steppin around out here. If we're being watched, our shit must look flaky enough as it is. Everybody keep a sharp eye and stay spread out."

After a time, Tucker found a pace that allowed everyone to keep up, and with each kilometer the walking became easier. Every half hour the litter bearers were changed. Occasionally, Clayborn used his good hand to help out when it was Douh's turn on the poles. Conroy had by now regained consciousness, moaning from time to time when the litter was juggled. Monroe tried keeping his mind off the pain by telling him stories.

The squad was nearing the end of the Plain of Reeds, but at their slow rate of travel, they wouldn't reach the village for another hour.

In the distance ahead, a column of black smoke rose above the treelines.

Chapter 27

The village looked like it was sucking itself in at the sight of him. Men and women working in the rice fields dropped what they were doing and streamed in from the paddies. Mothers and older sisters rushed to herd children and young siblings inside their homes. The village peeked from its doorways, watching Sau Ban approach from the west.

The village was quiet as night when Sau Ban carried the mortar tube and rucksack to the center of the village and stopped. Sau Ban's moves were deliberately slow while he shook the pack from his shoulders. When he dropped the mortar tube at his feet, the sound was like a broken bell echoing through the quiet village.

When he spoke, his loud voice cracked the stillness.

"The imperialists are coming back," he said, and began walking through the village, looking this way and that like he were inspecting troops. "The village must be evacuated."

An elderly man with a gray mustache and strands of hair hanging from his chin approached him from one of the huts. He pressed his hands together and bowed before speaking.

"We have done nothing. Why should we fear them?"

Sau Ban's eyes flared at the question, but he held his temper.

"Do you think the soldiers are stupid? One of your own led them into my ambush."

"But we had nothing to do with that. They have been here before and never harmed us."

"Am I a liar?" Sau Ban said.

Murmurs of excitement came from inside the huts. More faces began to poke from doorways.

"But we have done nothing," the old man repeated.

"Tell that to the Americans when your family is being killed in front of you!" Sau Ban barked. He was growing tired of the old man's belligerence. "Maybe you can tell them it is all a mistake and they will stop? The soldiers will take out their revenge nonetheless!" Sau Ban couldn't imagine why they wouldn't.

Sau Ban reached out and shook the old man by his chin whiskers, and a loud gasp came from those watching this show of disrespect.

"For the last time, uncle," Sau Ban said, drawing his face close to the old man's. "Clear the village. Run and hide in the trees. NOW!"

Women and children began to inch from doorways. They looked from neighbor to neighbor. Children old enough to understand what was being said clung to their parent's legs. Some began to cry. And then, as if a starting gun went off, the people bolted from their homes and out of the village.

Men called to their wives, and mothers screamed for children. The villagers fled out into the paddies with nothing but the clothes on their backs. Even the village livestock were drawn into the confusion. A black pig dashed through the crowd. He snorted and shouldered people aside as he went. Chickens cackled and flew every which way between the huts. The villagers first ran as a mob, then broke into small groups of families, each heading in separate directions for the treelines.

Sau Ban waved his pistol in the air, heightening the fear, charging behind everyone, screaming for them to move faster.

Tuan's mother was the only one who refused to flee with the rest. She dragged along behind Sau Ban, begging for news of her son. Only when the village was empty, and the terrified voices of its people were fading in the distance did Sau Ban acknowledge her presence. He spun on his heels and gazed down at her.

"Have you seen Tuan? Where is my son?"

Sau Ban knew, if nothing else, honor dictated he offer words of condolence.

"Your son died like a soldier," he said in a level voice.

Her face blanched at the words and her knees buckled. Only his hand gripping her arm kept her from falling. She was about to speak but he raised a hand to silence her. "Now listen to me. When the imperialists come, they must not find anything here of use to them, he said. "They will need water. I will destroy the water urns. They must not be allowed to find shelter here. The village is to be destroyed."

Her head rolled on her shoulders, and her body went slack.

Sau Ban held her steady, then gave her a shake. "Go to your home and gather what you can. The Americans will be coming soon. We must hurry."

She staggered back like she had been shoved. Her lips moved soundlessly over black, betel-nut-stained teeth. Then she turned and ran with a scream that followed her inside the house.

Sau Ban watched her go, then sprang into action. He sprinted to where the mortar tube lay and carried it to the far end of the village. Beside each hut were large clay urns for collecting rain water. Using the butt of the tube, he ran back and forth through the village smashing the urns. When he was finished, he ran inside one of the empty huts and found an oil lamp. He lit it and stepped out into the sunlight.

He stooped beside the first hut, and touched flame to dry wall. The fire caught quickly and in a matter of seconds the wall was engulfed. He darted to a hut on the other side of the dike and set it ablaze before moving on, putting fire to each in turn.

Behind him the village was consuming itself. Flames leapt high, pieces of charred palms fluttered skyward with the heat and smoke.

When he came to the last home, Sau Ban charged through the door and pulled up short.

A chair lay on its side by the table. Tuan's mother hung from the roof beam above, a strand of buffalo hide around her neck. Her toes stretched themselves, paddled the air below, and were then still. The crotch of her black satin pants was wet. Urine dripped from one foot and onto the dirt floor.

He had the distant memory of a woman hovering above the ground in much the same way. He could hear the sound of men laughing. French words being shouted in a slurred and ferocious sound. There had been fire then, too. He remembered how the woman glowed with it, the way shadows played on her face. Once more he could feel the powerful hands on his arms, lifting him, his small legs kicking to run from the horrible sight until he cried out her name.

Sau Ban backed out of the door. Rubbed his tired face and eyes. Around him, smoke and flames swirled through the village. He hurried back for his things. To his right, the roof beam of a blazing hut caved in. Cherry-red embers blew over him, stung his skin. Heat came in waves. Sweat glistened on his bare chest. He shouldered the rucksack and mortar tube, then ran from the village and into the trees.

While he waited he became aware of two things. The first was that the odds of landing any of the mortar rounds within the village were slim at best. Holding the tube with one hand while he dropped rounds into it with the other would not allow him to maintain a pattern of trajectory. If he hit the village once, he would be happy. After this, he knew, he would have no more use for the mortar, and the knowledge brought him to the second of his realizations: The Americans were going to kill him. Not here, he thought, but soon they will kill me. And in the last place they will ever expect me to be.

Sau Ban smiled inwardly at the thought. Despite what he had promised himself earlier, he was still making plans. Old habits die hard. But this one, he knew, would surely be his last. The long walk from the Dinh Ba Forest had allowed him plenty of time for thought. He now realized a warrior should not expect a long life. Thinking otherwise was foolish. To die for the cause of liberation, that was the greatest of honors. And to be able to choose the circumstances in which to receive that honor was a gift. He would not be taken by surprise. If he was going to die, then his death would be on his terms, the same way he had lived. He would orchestrate the time and place, use his cunning, his skills to their full advantage. He was now one man against them all, and he would fight until he could fight no more. Let the Americans kill him. They could only do it once, but he would take as many lives as possible before giving up his own. A man willing and eager to give his life for his beliefs was a force more powerful and threatening than anything the imperialists had at their disposal. In the end, he would be remembered as a hero. And while he waited for the soldiers to come back to Xon Dao, Sau Ban found himself growing anxious for these final hours to begin.

Chapter 28

By the time the squad reached the village, it was in ruins. The dried palms that once covered each home had burned so quickly that many of the corner poles still stood, charred and smoking, like remnants of a sparse forest rising above the smoldering ashes. With the exception of several white ducks swimming peacefully in a paddy nearby, and chickens pecking their way through the grit, the village was deserted.

Tuan's house had been the only one to survive the fire. A breeze had driven the flames in the other direction. Leon, walking point, entered the village shortly ahead of the squad. When the rest of them arrived, he was staring slack-jawed through the open doorway. Monroe moved passed him and turned Tuan's mother until they could see her swollen face.

He drew back in surprise. "Ain't this that guy's mother?" he said, and tilted his head in order to get a better look.

"Yes," Douh said, coming up behind Leon.

Leon withdrew from the sight. Bile choked in his throat, and he bent, spitting and coughing into the dirt and ashes outside. He reached for one of his canteens, but it was empty like the rest.

"What you think, Doe-doe? Spose she did this herself, or did she have a little help from Charlie Cong?" Monroe asked.

Tucker came up just then to see what the problem was. After he looked in the house, he and Douh exchanged glances, but neither of them made comment.

"And why the fuck would they burn the village if they were only after her?" Monroe mused.

The room seemed filled with questions for which no one had an answer. He walked back outside, and kicked at what had once been someone's table.

"And what happened to all the people?" Clayborn added after taking a good survey of the area. Traces of dried blood ran to his elbow. Some of the blood looked fresh.

Preacher was on his knees a short distance behind them. He kept arching and relaxing his back painfully.

For the last hundred meters or so, Conroy had been conscious. He kept babbling about a dog named Sadie giving birth. He was naming each pup as it was born. He'd run through over twenty names.

"Must'a been one hell of a dog," Monroe said to no one in particular. He wet one end of his towel with the last of his canteen water and began wiping Conroy's face and forehead.

Tucker checked the time. It was now 1500. The going had been extremely slow so far. Everyone was exhausted, and Clayborn and Preacher could hardly put one foot in front of the other. Neither complained, but judging by the expressions on their faces their wounds were hurting them something terrible.

If not for the wounded, Tucker knew the squad could make it to Tan Tru by nightfall. But at the rate they were going, it would take them twice that long: if they could even muster the strength to do it at all. His own arms ached so badly from carrying Conroy that it was difficult to open and close his hands. His legs felt weak and rubbery. Tucker suspected everyone else was in the same condition. Something different had to be done.

"Leon," Tucker said. "Come on over here. There's some shit we need to talk about."

Like he'd been walking towards the edge of something, Leon suddenly jumped forward and dropped to his knees. He started digging with his hands.

"We gotta bury her," he choked.

Dirt flew between his legs in a dog-like fashion. For several minutes he did this until his strength gave out. He then sat back on his heels and looked up at the sky. His grimy cheeks sucked and billowed the air. When he finally faced them he saw everyone was looking at him.

"This place," he said, shaking his head in a barely noticeable way. "This place keeps getting worse."

Tucker moved forward and knelt beside him. The rest of the squad turned away.

"I can't do this anymore. I don't wanna see any more dead people, Tuck. I just don't wanna see any more dead people."

Tucker spoke softly into his face so that only Leon could hear. "I know, buddy. We're gonna get home, Leon. Keep thinking about home. Okay? Don't quit on me now."

As quickly as his breakdown had come, Leon seemed to gather back the pieces of himself. He pulled away and wiped his nose on his arm, then took a few deep breaths to clear his head. When he looked, he was happy to see that none of the men were watching. No one spoke.

But Monroe was already on the move. "Gimme a hand here, Doe-doe," he said, drew his bayonet and entered the hut. After a brief struggle to cut her down without dropping her, Tuan's mother lay on the floor of her home, and Monroe sent Douh back out for the entrenching tool.

The dirt floor of the hut was packed like concrete and Monroe had to use the pick side of the tool until he could break through to soft dirt. But he never complained.

"Could I do that?"

Monroe looked up from where he was pushing the shovel into the dirt with his boot. Leon stood in the doorway, sunlight framing him.

"Sure, my man," Monroe said, straightening up. "I could use a break."

Leon took the entrenching tool and dug, piling the dirt neatly to the side of the hole.

"One summer, me and Tuck had a job digging graves back home."

"That right?" Monroe said casually.

"Yeah," Leon said. "We got a hundred bucks a grave."

"Not bad. How long one a them things take you?"

"Eight hours. But we only got to dig one."

"I guess that be all right."

Leon stopped for a moment and shot him a curious look.

"I mean," Monroe said, and the cleft in his chin showed a little. "If there ain't no graves being dug, then I guess ain't nobody doing no dying."

Leon looked back down at the hole, and nodded. "That's a nice way to think of it, Monroe."

Monroe lit a Salem and edged it to the side of his mouth. "There it is, my man," he said. "Here, let me spell you on this for a while."

In another half hour they had a hole large enough to place her in. Leon spread his poncho over the bottom of the grave, and together they lay Tuan's mother on it. Ten minutes later she was buried.

"You know much about the Bible, Monroe?"

"Just who wrote it." He smiled.

"Ask Preach if he could come in here, will you?"

Monroe stepped outside, and a moment later returned with Preacher.

"There's a book in the Bible," Leon said without looking up. "Ecclesiastes. You know it?"

"I know of it, Leon."

"There's this one chapter in it my mom always liked. Something about how there is a time for things."

"Hey, yeah," Preacher said. "My dad reads that at funerals all the time."

"Can you remember any of the verses?"

"Yeah, I can remember some of it. Let's see. There is a time for everything, and a season for every activity under heaven. A time to be born, and a time to die. A time to kill and a time to heal."

Preacher paused and stared off across the room.

"That all you can think of?" Leon asked.

"No, there's a bunch of them. A time to weep, and a time to laugh. That's one. Yeah, and a time for war, and a time for peace. I wish I could remember them all. It's a real pretty thing when my old man reads it."

"It's good enough, Preach. Thanks."

They were about to leave when Monroe turned and knelt by the side of the grave. With his finger he drew a peace sign on top of the dirt mound.

Once the squad was gathered outside again, they formed a loose huddle around Conroy's litter, each of them continuing to look this way and that, each knowing that whoever had set fire to the village might still be somewhere in the area.

Tucker ran through the details of the information Douh had revealed to him about Sau Ban.

"You mean all this is because of him?" Monroe said.

Douh didn't like the way Monroe said *him*. He was suddenly aware of being different than the rest. It made him nervous enough that he moved back from the circle a bit.

Tucker also caught the inflection in Monroe's voice, and moved quickly to stop it. "Doe-doe couldn't have known what was going to happen anymore than we could, Monroe. If anything, he's in more danger than any of us. Think about it."

Monroe lit a Salem and held the filter between his teeth, then gestured at the surroundings, at the wounded. "You telling me some crazy bastard's done all this just because he wants to kill Doe-doe?"

"I saw him in the forest, Monroe," Douh said. He found it difficult to speak, was afraid of drawing too much attention to himself.

"Her son was with us," Tucker said. "Think it's just coincidence?"

Monroe peeked back through the doorway and blew smoke through his nostrils disgustedly. "I don't think nothing anymore. The fucking Nam, man."

Agreement murmured all around, and Tucker sought to change the subject back to the matters at hand.

"We need to take a vote," he said. "The way I figure it, we're gonna need to get Conroy and the rest some medical attention sooner than we thought. I don't know about everybody else, but I ain't so sure I can carry him much farther."

He paused and looked from one face to the other. No one said anything. Leon kicked at the dirt. Monroe stared down at Conroy.

"We're gonna have to go for help," Tucker said. "It's the only way."

Monroe kept his head down, but nodded slowly. "What you thinking, Tucker?"

Tucker cast a glance around the group before speaking. "What if a couple of us was to head out for the camp? Two men could make a lot of time. Maybe be there in three hours. These guys would be on a dust-off a lot sooner than if we all tried getting back together."

Monroe looked up from Conroy. "So who's gonna go?"

"That's what we need to vote on."

"I ain't leaving Conroy," Monroe said. "The rest of you decide. I'm staying here."

Leon scuffed his boot in the dirt again, then looked around at Preacher and Clayborn. "You go, Tuck. Me and Monroe can handle things here all right."

"You sure, Leon? I could stay," Tucker said.

Leon shot him a weary smile, and shook his head. "Naw, you go.

Be honest with you, I don't wanna be the first one back answering questions."

Tucker nodded and returned the smile. "I'd forgotten about—"

"Tell them it was my idea."

Everyone turned to look at Clayborn.

"I'm the highest-ranking man here. Captain Decker's the only one we have to worry about, and he's on R&R. If Boyle gives you any shit, you tell him he can deal with me when I get back. Unless I miss my guess, he won't do anything but blow smoke for a while. If you want, tell Boyle I said he can kiss my ass."

"Damn, Lieutenant," Tucker grinned. "I don't think I better say that to him."

"Fine," Clayborn said. "I'd rather do it myself anyway. You two had better move out if you're going."

"There it is," Tucker said, eyeing Douh, who looked relieved to learn he would be traveling with Tucker.

"How much water you guys got?" Tucker asked, and he looked around at the broken urns.

"We got two full canteens between us," Monroe said.

Tucker tossed him what remained of his. "You got water, Doe-doe?"

"One full, Tucker."

"All right. We can share it." Tucker checked the time. "If help isn't here by around 2000. . .well I guess that means something happened and you're gonna have to make it on your own."

"You ready, Doe-doe?"

Douh nodded.

"Okay," Tucker said. "Guess we better haul—"

The first mortar landed so far out in the paddies that none of the men heard it coming.

"Incoming!" Tucker screamed, and dove to the ground a second before the next mortar fell, blowing rice plants and mud high over the paddies and across the village.

Monroe shielded Conroy with his body, covered his own helmet with his hands. Everyone else except for Clayborn and Tucker ran for the edge of the dike, hitting the water like schoolboys diving into a shallow swimming hole.

Clayborn was on his knees, looking to the trees where he saw a puff of smoke signaling the launching of a new round.

"I got a fix on the bastard, Tucker," he screamed, balancing his weapon awkwardly over the forearm of his wounded hand. He fired in short bursts. Now and then a red tracer zipped into the trees right where he was aiming.

For his part, Tucker heard only the white hot crack of the explosions, and each one drew him tighter into that hated fetal position until he became as useless to himself as if he really were a baby.

Clayborn was doing his best to load in another clip when the last mortar fell close enough to splatter him with mud and water, but nothing else.

Everyone stayed where they were and waited. The ducks, scattered by the explosions, began to quack from separate parts of the paddy. In the time it took for the ducks to reform, Tucker had uncurled himself and looked around to see if anyone was hurt.

"We got movement in the treeline!" Leon yelled from his position behind the dike.

"Over here, too!" Clayborn said, pointing in the opposite direction.

Tucker tried looking everywhere at once, and each place he looked, he saw people stepping out of the trees and into the paddies. "Hold your fire! Hold your fire!" he ordered, then lifted to his knees for a better view.

Far out on a dike a man wearing a pair of gray shorts walked towards them. He waved a straw conical hat above his head, yelling at them.

"What's he saying, Doe-doe?" Tucker called over his shoulder.

"He is the head man of the village. He says not to shoot him. He is friendly. He wants to speak with us."

When the old man finally stood in the center of the wasted village, he could do nothing except stare at the devastation.

"Find out what he knows, Doe-doe," Tucker said.

Around the treeline perimeter the villagers waited in small groups. In the distance, the men heard the cries of small children.

Douh pressed his hands together and exchanged bows with the man, then the two of them squatted on their haunches and the old man spoke rapidly, waving wildly in all directions, sounding more angry with each gesture. Douh finally offered him a cigarette to shut him up, then stood to relay the news.

"He says that Sau Ban has done all this alone and now run away. He has been terrorizing the village for a long time. The old man wants to be rid of him, but they are not soldiers. Without their homes they have nothing but the land until they can rebuild. They are afraid if they stay here that Sau Ban will return and kill them all."

"Ask him what he wants from us," Tucker said

Douh did, and after another long tirade from the old man, he faced Tucker once more.

"He wants to know if they can come with us," Douh answered.

When Monroe finished counting the villagers who were lined up behind them and ready to move out with the squad for Tan Tru, Tucker asked how many there were.

"Forty-one," Monroe answered, shaking his head. "Ain't this some shit? We set out for orchids and come back with refugees."

"How's Conroy?"

"He's hanging in there. The mamasans are tending to him. Every time I try and do something for him they shoo me away. They won't even let me help carry the man."

Tucker looked back down the line. Preacher and Clayborn balanced together atop a water buffalo led by a young boy.

"Sure wish we had a picture of this," he said.

"That ain't no lie," Monroe said. "Gotta see this place to believe it."

Chapter 29

After a solid hour of walking, Tucker finally called for a five-minute break inside a treeline. Douh informed the villagers, then came back and sat across from Tucker, who was slumped against a tree trunk. The shade of the treeline was welcome, though the air was still and heavy. Overhead, Douh could see the tops of the palms waving gently, but none of the breeze passed over where he and Tucker rested.

Douh felt like talking. Something to take his mind off thinking about Sau Ban and the safety of being back inside the camp.

"A question, Tucker."

"Shoot," Tucker said.

"When you were a boy, did you ever think of doing what you are doing now?"

Tucker stared ahead and laughed without smiling. "Me an' Leon used to play Army down the railroad tracks back home. We'd go at it for hours. Take turns being the enemy. Nobody could die like Leon could. He always had these great last words. Corny as hell."

"What is corny?"

"You know. Dramatic. Like in John Wayne movies. Stupid shit."

"America is a strange place where children play war. In my country, we take it more serious. War is what we are. It is what we know from the time we are small."

"The ying and yang of it, Doe-doe."

"You know this?"

"Not much. There was this guy who used to come in the station where Leon worked. Schoolteacher from another town. Sometimes he'd talk about how things are balanced. Darkness and light. Love and hate. Life and death. Stuff like that. He told us once that Satan was necessary for God to exist. Even He needed the balance."

"Did you believe him?"

"Seems like he's right. Don't matter what I believe."

"In my school," Douh said. "I used to study the globe. I would look to your side of the world, at your country, then spin the globe back to mine. Do you know you come from nearly the exact opposite side of the world?"

"Never gave it much thought."

"The ying and the yang. America is rich. We are poor. Perhaps we provide the balance."

"There it is."

Tucker bummed a smoke and he and Douh lit up together, both puffing in quiet contentment for a spell.

"You'd think he'd give up after while," Tucker said.

"Sau Ban?"

Tucker nodded.

"No," Douh murmured. "Sau Ban is a true believer. I have betrayed the cause. Upset the balance. For that he hates me even more than he hates you. There is nothing he will not do. He is *liet sy*. A martyr. Even his own life is without value until all *thong miao* have been chased from our country."

"I don't know the word."

Douh peeked at him sheepishly. "*Thong miao* is what we call Americans."

"What's it mean?"

Douh looked to his feet. "Gooks."

"There it is." Tucker laughed.

"What will you do when you go home?" Douh asked.

"I wish I knew."

"Your Uncle Sam says thank you very much for the help. Now you can go back to what you were doing?"

Tucker didn't have an answer for that.

"Do you think it will end?"

"The war?" Tucker said.

"Yes."

"Someday. It can't go on forever."

"You are wrong. Inside here," Douh said, and pressed his hand to his forehead. "Inside here it will never end. The ying and the yang. I will still be living it. You will be in America remembering it."

"And if I never think of it again? Then what?"

Douh smiled and juggled his hands. "Then a part of you will be out of balance."

Tucker considered this for a time, gazing through the trees, fixing his eyes on something far out in the paddies. In a few minutes, he checked his watch, then pulled himself to his feet. "Part of me's been out of balance my whole life, Doe-doe. Ain't nothing new about that."

The sun was near the horizon. Shadows in the treelines were growing longer and casting themselves out into the paddies. The best anyone could figure, they still had an hour of walking left. The fear of booby traps slowed them more than anything, and each time they were forced to enter a new treeline their pace dropped considerably.

Soon the paddies were awash in a smudged gray. To the west the orange sky dwindled like an old fire until a hood of darkness fell over the countryside. There wasn't anything left for them to do now but concentrate on putting one foot in front of the other on the narrow dikes.

Chapter 30

Higgins was back. Just before the road closed at 1700, Higgins returned on a supply truck coming from Dong Tam. He'd been gone a little over a week, but other than a wide strip of gauze plastered over his nose, and two of the blackest eyes Boyle had ever seen, he didn't look or sound much worse for wear.

"You should have seen the nurses," Higgins said, and he scooped up the cribbage hand Boyle was dealing out on his desk in the CQ shack. "Round-eyed American girls, Top. I had a blue-veiner the whole time."

Boyle scanned his cards, only half listening. At that moment he was so happy to have Higgins back to play cribbage with again that he was giving serious thought to playing the game for once without cheating.

"Round-eyes, huh?" Boyle said in passing.

"Yep. Gorgeous. Every last one of them. Blondes, Top. You should of seen them. There was this one that did things to a set of jungle fatigues like you wouldn't believe."

"You get laid?"

"No, but . . ."

"Then I don't wanna hear about it," Boyle grumbled, opening his desk drawer and plopping down a half-empty bottle of Old Grandad on the desk between them. "Be my guest," he said.

Higgins eyed the bottle with a surging pain in his nose. The last thing he wanted was to have a drunken fit of vomiting later.

"I'll pass, Top."

"Suit yourself," Boyle said. He unscrewed the cap and tipped the bottle to his lips. Boyle smacked his lips in a breathless exhale before setting the bottle back down. Higgins hadn't been stoned since the night of the mortar attack, and though he'd never lit up in front of Top, he wondered, given his present condition, if Boyle would mind.

"I'd rather have a smoke, Top."

Boyle stared at his cards and fumbled a pack of Luckies from his shirt pocket, tossing them on the desk.

"I got my own," Higgins said. He reached carefully in the leg pocket of his pants, then held up a joint the size of his little finger. "Would it be okay, Top?"

Boyle glanced over the top of his cards, then did a double take. "Is that—"

"Yeah. Would it be all right?"

"This is company headquarters, damn it!"

"I'd feel a lot better, Top. Captain Decker is on R&R. Who's gonna know?"

"I'll know! That shit's against regulations!" Boyle kept his eyes on the joint and reached for the bottle. "I won't have it!"

"But you're in here drinking."

"That's different," Boyle snapped, and took a swig.

"Captain Decker wouldn't think so."

"The captain can go pound sand up his ass!"

"My nose hurts, Top. I can't concentrate on the game."

Boyle stared at the bandage beneath Higgins' glasses, at his two black eyes. He was a pitiful sight.

"What if somebody comes in?"

"You're in charge here," Higgins answered calmly. "Tell whoever it is to stay out. Come on, Top. Be a pal. It's Christmas."

Boyle ran his eyes over the room. Gloria's picture still hung on the wall, the hole in her smile lent her face a stupid expression, which was the only reason Boyle kept her there. Only that morning he'd written her a scathing letter wherein he'd called her every foul name he knew. None of it would help his cause of course, but it did make him feel better.

"All right, Higgins," he sighed. "Just this once. But only because it's Christmas."

"Ata boy, Top!" Higgins said.

With a deft movement, he flipped open his lighter and lit the joint.

Boyle watched him with a wary eye, like he might suddenly take on a new shape, or somehow look different.

After holding in the smoke for what seemed to Boyle a ridiculous amount of time, Higgins exhaled loudly and shot him a silly grin.

"Now I got something for you," he said. He rushed into his office and returned with one hand held behind his back, then slid a bottle of Jack Daniels on the desk.

"I picked it up in Dong Tam for you, Top. Merry Christmas."

Boyle's face lit up like a child's. He took the bottle, held it in both hands, and examined the black label as if it were a family heirloom. "And a merry one it's gonna be, too!" he said. He unscrewed the cap and waved it beneath his nose like a connoisseur.

Higgins took a long pull on the joint and leaned his head on the back of the chair. Boyle was all right, once you got to know him. He blew a stream of smoke to the ceiling, wondering how Christmas had gone back home.

Meanwhile, Boyle rummaged through his desk drawer for a shot glass, then poured himself two finger's worth and tossed it into his mouth with a smooth motion. The taste of good whiskey flared in his throat, and he took a quick breath to heighten it. Not even the fact that 2nd squad was missing could ruin his Christmas, now. The squad had made radio contact once the day before, so he knew they were alive or at least had been. But as to what they were up to, no one had a clue. And after giving it some thought, Boyle had just about convinced himself it was Clayborn's ass—not his, anyway. Captain Decker couldn't hold him responsible. He hadn't been on the runaway LP.

Boyle re-filled the shot glass with one hand and gathered his cards in the other. "Now, Higgins. Let's you and me play some cribbage."

They played the hand while Higgins continued to toke on the joint until only a tiny part of it remained. When he popped the roach in his mouth and swallowed it, Boyle stared at him in wonder.

"What'd you do that for?"

"Habit." Higgins smiled back.

A field telephone sitting on the far corner of Boyle's desk suddenly rang. Boyle held the handset to his ear.

"Charlie Company. Boyle."

Boyle listened, now and then snapping off a "Yes, sir!" or a "roger that!"

When he finally hung up the receiver, he was no longer happy.

"Fuckin ARVNs. Fuckin gooks."

"What is it, Top?"

"That was the major. The dinks are hitting an ARVN compound near the Cambodian border. The major wants Charlie Company saddled and ready to move out in fifteen." Boyle ran a hand over his mouth and paced a tight circle behind the desk. "The captain's gone. Who's senior officer?"

Higgins looked at him thoughtfully for a moment. "Clayborn."

"Clayborn! Who the fuck knows where he is! Next?"

"Lieutenant Bradshaw."

"Find Bradshaw and tell him to get every available man out on the road and ready for the choppers. ASAP!"

Chapter 31

"Hear that?" Tucker said to Monroe, who was standing close behind him on the dike.

Monroe nodded in the darkness. "Choppers. Lots of 'em."

Strung in a line behind them, half of the villagers were standing in the open paddies, the other half still waiting in the treeline to come out.

The mingled thumping of rotor blades grew steadily louder. Suddenly the night sky over Tan Tru lit with one brilliant white star. Soon another joined it, then another, until there were twelve in all as the choppers lit their belly lights and descended to the camp below.

"Somebody done stepped in it somewhere," Monroe said.

"Pass word for everybody to get down," Tucker said. "If they come this way and happen to see us down here like this all hell will break loose."

In the time it took for the frightened villagers to hop in the paddies and hunker beside the dikes, the noise of the choppers lifting Charlie Company from the camp rattled through the paddies. Next, twelve Huey slicks barreled out of the darkness at treetop level. They were flying in line and the sound was deafening. Their rotor wash blew conical hats into the paddies in a rush of mechanical wind.

"Wonder who's getting the Christmas present?" Monroe said in a near normal voice once the choppers had passed. There didn't seem to be much use of trying to hide the fact they were out there: not with the villagers and a water buffalo splashing along behind them.

Christmas. Tucker had forgotten. He stared in the direction of the choppers. He wished he'd been able to see what company it was leaving in such a hurry.

Tucker had been wanting to apologize to someone: to say he

knew everything was his fault. But the moment had never seemed right. They were almost home, and who knew how bad it would be when they got back. Technically, he didn't think the squad would be classified as AWOL, and they hadn't deserted. They'd merely pulled their own operation. He gave the idea some thought.

"I'm sorry I talked you guys into this shit, Monroe. I want you to know that," he finally said.

"Hey, Tucker. A man does what he does. We went out together, and we fucked up together. Coulda been a lot worse, you ask me. There's enough blame to go around. We made it, my man. It's all that matters, now. So, Merry Christmas."

"Yeah, Monroe. Merry Christmas to you, too."

Tucker chewed his bottom lip. He appreciated Monroe's words, but they couldn't change what he felt about himself. He thought about Clayborn, about how easy it was to fuck things up in this place. There were plenty of ways to die here without looking for new ones. Thinking back on it just then, he couldn't seem to re-member why the idea of getting the orchid had seemed so impor-tant in the first place. He hadn't been trying to prove anything. It was more to see if they could pull it off, a lark, and Tucker knew they all should have known better. He flashed on something Mon-roe had said last week about guilt. Monroe had said they were all going to have a measure of it. Now he knew Monroe had been right. This was not the sort of place that would leave any of them untouched by that measure. He'd been in-country long enough to know that when a man started taking the place for granted, bad things happened, people got hurt. He'd allowed himself to grow casual to the war, and he was sorry and saddened. That was it, Tucker figured, that was where the guilt came from. The life-long second guess. The recurring what if. At that moment it was too much to consider. He held in a slow deep breath, then whistled it through his lips.

"We gotta think how we're going to approach the camp. It's right on the other side of that treeline. We can't just walk in from the paddies without letting them know."

"Let's take 'em back the way we came. Follow the river."

"Most likely there's gonna be an LP by the river," Tucker mused.

"We'll have to send someone on ahead to let them know that friendlies are coming," Monroe said. "Shit, man, that's the least of our worries."

"I'm just trying to keep anything else from going wrong, is all."

"I'm with ya, brother. We'll be home before you now it."

As it turned out, Monroe and Tucker had both been right. There was an LP posted by the river, but like Monroe had predicted, they didn't have any problem making contact with them. Monroe had gone ahead, warning the LP of the approaching throng. The LP then radioed the camp and told them to make ready to accept—the cherry using the radio had been too green to call them anything else—forty-one prisoners.

"They're refugees, peckerhead," Monroe said at the FNG's mistake. But he didn't have him correct it. Prisoners sounded better anyway, and Monroe figured it might buy the squad some time before the hard questions started getting asked.

But there weren't any. Not that night, anyway.

The battalion CO, Colonel Hacker, was away on a three day R&R up in Saigon. In his absence, Major George, the battalion executive officer, was left in charge. At the moment, he was involved in a high-decibel, low-stakes Christmas poker game in the officer's mess, leaving word he should only be disturbed in case of emergency, and fortunately for the squad, no one else in the camp considered refugees to be in that category.

Douh was placed in charge of the refugees who were taken to the open-sided schoolhouse that battalion had built for the village. They huddled under its corrugated metal roof, making themselves comfortable until morning. For the time being, there wasn't anything more to be done with them.

Everyone else accompanied the wounded to the aid-station where the medics tended to their injuries. A medevac chopper was called and soon on its way to take them to the hospital at Can Tho.

While the camp's medics worked, Tucker, Leon, and Monroe huddled around them like anxious mothers. Everyone knew Conroy and Clayborn would not be coming back. For them the war was over, and the minutes spent waiting for the medevac took on a sense of immediacy.

Clayborn had asked a medic for a pen and something to write on. He spent a long time scribbling left-handed on a piece of unlined stationery. When he'd finished, he shoved the note to Tucker.

"It says the squad was acting under my orders. I'm out of this now," Clayborn said. "They can't do anything to me. I'm quitting the service, Tucker. There won't be a career left to court-martial."

"Good for you, Lieutenant," Tucker grinned. He was pleased to learn Clayborn was getting out.

For a few seconds their eyes locked. Each looked like there were something more to say, but then the moment went flat.

"You write us. Okay?" Tucker finally said.

Clayborn only nodded.

They shook with their left hands, and Clayborn lay back on the cot, staring at the silver light shade hanging above him. Nothing more was said.

Tucker looked to where Preacher and Leon were talking. Preacher lay face-down on a cot. A medic was cleaning his wounds with a large cue-tip. They didn't look so bad now that they were cleaned up.

"I hope you get to go home, Preach," Tucker said, though he knew Preacher would most likely return to finish his tour.

"That's two of us, Tucker."

"If you do, make sure you stay in touch. You ain't so far from where me and Leon are from. We'll have a party when we all get back."

"I'll be waiting," Preacher said. He grimaced at the swabbing being done to his back.

Conroy wasn't doing any talking. He had been given a shot of morphine shortly after the medics got their hands on him. The medics had him swathed in fresh bandages, and there was a higher-than-hell smile on his face.

Monroe sat across the room on a wheeled examination stool, twirling an unlit cigarette between his fingers because the medics told him he couldn't smoke.

A medic was staring at Tucker.

"What the hell is that thing on your chest?"

Tucker looked down at the wad of pus on his chest, which smelled faintly of vinegar. Tucker had been noticing the odor for some time.

"Let me get something on that," the medic said.

Tucker waited while the medic cleaned the tattoo and dabbed on ointment.

"You get back in here tomorrow."

"Sure," Tucker said. "First thing."

In the distance they could hear the medevac chopper pass once over the far end of the camp. And after a few more of the usual good-byes—write, keep your head down—Clayborn, Preacher, and Conroy were carried to the waiting dust-off and loaded on board. And just that quickly they were gone.

At the edge of Charlie's company area, Monroe pulled up short. The place was too quiet. There weren't any radios playing, no lights burning in any of the hootches. The only building that appeared to be inhabited was the CQ, where soft yellow light shown from its front door.

"Looks like it was us we saw leaving on them choppers," Monroe said. "Think maybe Boyle went with them?"

"If he did it would be the first time," Tucker said.

"So what do we do?" Leon asked.

"Fuck it. Let's go take our ass-chewing and get it over with," Tucker answered. "I wanna get some sleep."

They waited outside the CQ for a while, listening.

"Hey," Monroe whispered. "Sounds like Higgins is back."

Inside the place they could hear Higgins laughing, and the sound of Boyle coughing violently.

Monroe turned as if to speak, but Tucker shushed him.

"You took too big of a hit, Top," Higgins was saying. "Just take a small toke and hold it in for a bit. You'll get used to it."

Monroe nearly screamed, but managed to hold his voice down. "Motherfucker's getting stoned!"

Higgins' voice floated through the doorway again.

"That's it, Top. Now, let it out."

Boyle exhaled loudly. "I don't feel nothing."

"Give it a while, Top. Do another."

"Come on," Monroe said, and made a move for the door. "Let's go in there and catch him in the act."

Higgins had his feet propped on the desktop, grinning at Boyle, who sat across from him, eyes closed, sucking on the last of the joint. It took a moment or two before either of them realized the three men had entered the office.

Boyle's eyes were glassy and pink, the half-empty bottle of Jack Daniels sat on one corner of the desk. Boyle made a move to stand,

then flopped back into the chair. He still had the joint held between his thumb and index. He looked at it, then at everyone else
in the place. He mugged a dumbfounded expression, like he was
having a difficult time understanding how all these things were
connected.

"Higgins, my man," Monroe said just then. "What you all doing,
brother?"

Higgins grinned as widely as the tape and gauze over his nose
and cheeks would allow.

"Gettin' light, Monroe. Ain't that so, Top?"

Boyle tried standing again, with the same result as his previous
attempt. The strong weed was mixing well with the whiskey. He
didn't have a name for what he felt, but it was in no way unpleas-
ant. He couldn't seem to gather enough thoughts to make a statement: though he figured the situation called for one. He was suddenly aware that everyone was watching him, and at last his brows
knitted together with a thought.

"Hey. Where the hell have you guys been?"

Monroe stepped forward and took the joint from Boyle's fingers. After a toke he handed it back.

"Looking for flowers," Monroe answered, dragoning smoke from
his nose.

Boyle examined the joint as if it were an artifact. "Oh," he said,
then chuckled: "Did you find any?"

"A few," Monroe said, peeking at Leon and Tucker.

By now, Boyle felt like he might melt into the chair. The room
seemed much larger than he could remember. The three soldiers
standing across the room were difficult for him to focus on. He
knew each of their names, but at the moment he couldn't call a
one of them to mind. He stared back with a vacant smile. It was
the best he could do.

"Flowers. . .?" Higgins asked.

Monroe patted him on the shoulder. "Not now, my man. We need
some sleep. We're gonna leave you two to your party." He faced
Boyle again. "Merry Christmas, Top."

Boyle grinned back like an idiot. "Joy to the world," he said and
began to laugh.

He was still laughing when Monroe led Tucker and Leon from
the office.

Douh was waiting for them in the hootch when they arrived. Bastard sat on the floor at his feet, nibbling a C-ration cookie. When the three men entered the hootch, Bastard scrambled up the center pole of the room and stayed there. In the squad's absence, someone had arranged a small hammock-like roost for him from the fabric of a parachute flare, and Bastard settled in, as if for the night.

Tucker sat down heavily on his cot. He wanted to take his boots off, but the thought of bending over to unlace them seemed like more effort than it was worth. He sank to his back and the air left his lips in a sigh.

"Them people get their shit squared away, Doe-doe?" he asked softly.

"Yes."

Tucker's eyes fluttered shut. "God, I'm tired," he said after a moment. And he went to sleep.

Douh tugged Tucker's boots and wet socks from his feet, then tossed a poncho liner over him. He padded to the rear of the hootch and lit a smoke, gazing at the stars, happy to be alive.

Chapter 32

Sau Ban stood knee-deep in a pocket of backwater on the river, listening to the whispers and rustle of the guard changing on the LP a short distance away. After ten minutes he heard nothing more. He knew a man trying to stay awake would be adjusting himself from time to time in order to keep from becoming too comfortable. This guard wasn't. When he was sure the man had gone back to sleep, Sau Ban inched forward through the nipa palm on elbows and knees, quietly finding the tunnel and dropping into it.

He didn't know what to expect on the other end, maybe a trap, but the fact the entrance was still there indicated the Americans had yet to discover Tay Ninh's tunnel. They would have blown it by now. Destroyed it like they destroyed everything else they didn't understand.

The time was close to midnight when he came under the gaping hole in the tunnel's roof. Nothing had changed. The empty artillery box was still partially covering the hole, and he lay on his back for a few minutes, breathing in the fresh air. Sau Ban became more at ease with himself. There was nothing to stand in his way. Only wait for the first hour before dawn when the camp is quiet and sleeping.

He crawled for another half hour. At first he wasn't sure what to make of the situation. He expected the exit to be open, the way he had left it. It wasn't, and he grew wary. The trap door was back in place, no light showed between the cracks, and everything was quiet. He listened for sounds of movement. None came. Sau Ban raised his hands, pressed on the underside of the hatch. It gave way easily. The bureau was arranged to one side of the hole. In its place someone had covered the opening with a woven reed mat. A neighbor, perhaps. After the dead black air of the tunnel, the inside of the dark house looked bright in comparison.

Sau Ban eased himself from the pit, his pistol at the ready, but he was alone in the room. He located the oil lamp on the table and carried it to the bunker. Empty. Questions were everywhere. Could Tay Ninh be alive? If not, who covered the hole; who found her in the bunker? And if alive, where was she? While he pondered this last thought, he hurried to the door, opened it a crack, then peeked his head out. Nothing. He looked out the back window. The camp was quiet. In a few hours it wouldn't matter: none of it would. He made himself comfortable in Tay Ninh's hammock, and fell into a light sleep, the pistol resting on his chest.

There were cat-like footsteps on the floor. Sau Ban's eyes were open in an instant and his hand went to the pistol. Whoever was there, they went quickly to the open hole, then turned back the way they had come. Outside, he could hear whispering, and the sound of someone hurrying away.

That familiar feeling entered his chest once more, the tightness and pressure, the struggle to breathe. He lit the oil lamp and searched quickly for something he had seen on a previous visit. There it was, in the corner, a rice knife. He blew out the light and ran his fingers over the long, dogleg-shaped blade, cutting himself. He tasted his blood. It was nearly time to go. He dropped to the floor and began doing push-ups, not counting, but doing them until he could feel a good burning in his chest and arms. He did squat thrusts until his legs burned as well. With the knife over his head, he made slashing motions, spinning through the room, his tongue clicking with each thrust. His pistol lay on the table, and he went for it, but stopped short. He would go in armed with only the knife. A warrior to the end. The vision of being inside the camp caused his shoulders to quiver at the rush of adrenaline it would bring.

On the crawl back to the hole in the tunnel's ceiling, Sau Ban let his anger build with each scrape and gouge the walls laid on his skin. He crawled faster, smelling the sweetness of the fresh air ahead.

It had been lights-out in the CQ for some time. Higgins had long since gone to bed, leaving Boyle, face down and asleep on the desktop. He was having the strangest dream, not the least of which was that it all seemed to be in color.

He dreamt of being in a bright room full of men who looked exactly like him. A beautiful woman suddenly entered the room wearing a red gown that swirled languidly. Her lovely black hair flailed as if from a sharp breeze. All heads turned to look. Then she pointed, beckoning to a man who was he, but not him, and the dream ended when his bowels woke him with a rolling growl.

Boyle wasn't aware of what time it might be, where he might be, or who he might be. All his thoughts seemed to have a layer of fur around them. But he had to shit: that much he knew. It took some doing to get his feet under him, and when he was finally able to stand without holding onto the desk, he grabbed his flashlight and wobbled for the latrine.

On the other end of the camp Sau Ban was coming out of the tunnel. He crouched behind a stack of ammo boxes long enough to get his bearings, then set off for Charlie Company by dodging among the camp's shadows.

Despite having a flashlight, Boyle managed to get himself turned around, and for a few paces he was heading the wrong way. By the time he got straightened out and moving in the right direction, Sau Ban was crouching in front of the latrine, trying to decide which hootch to go in first. Sau Ban heard Boyle's stumbling footsteps on the path ahead, and, thinking only of concealment, he inched open the latrine's door and slipped inside.

When Boyle tripped into the side of the latrine, Sau Ban knew the man was drunk, and he relaxed a bit, backing into a shadowed corner, waiting for him to settle in.

Boyle wasn't sure if he didn't need to vomit more than anything, and he braced himself, his face hanging over the putrid hole, before turning to drop his pants. A second later he plopped onto the hole with the sound of a tired old man.

Sau Ban could sense heat rising to his skin. His breathing went shallow.

The realization that someone was standing in the corner gradually made its way through the fuzz of Boyle's muddled thoughts.

"Hey," Boyle said, his chest hiccoughing the word.

Sau Ban froze. An arm muscle began to cramp.

"Hey!" Boyle raised his voice. "In the corner. What's the problem?"

The air in Sau Ban's lungs felt hot, tight about his face.

Boyle fumbled for his flashlight.

"You gotta problem?"

He hit the switch a split second before Sau Ban swung the rice knife with such force it cut through Boyle's skull with no more effort than if it had been a ripe fruit. When Sau Ban wiggled the blade free, Boyle slumped into the wall, his hand still holding the flashlight, its beam shining levelly across the two remaining holes.

Sau Ban clipped the flashlight to the waistband of his shorts and was out of the place in an instant. He darted over to 1st platoon's hootch and slid partway under it. Above him someone turned in their sleep, the legs of the cot inched this way and that on the wood floor. A voice spoke. Every second of his life seemed to gather in a pinwheel rush of images. Providence was offering him one last chance to kill the traitor. For the voice coming through the floor above him was Douh's, talking in his sleep.

Sau Ban slipped quietly onto the steps and made his way inside the hootch. Douh mumbled once more in the background. Sau Ban cocked his head at the sound and started for it.

Bastard was awake, and the new odor that Sau Ban brought to the hootch caused him to leap up and down in his roost and screech like he were being chased by a snake.

Heads popped up in the starlit darkness filtering in through the screens.

Sau Ban stepped forward and swung at the first silhouette he could see. He felt the blade find its mark. A man's voice cried out. Sau Ban swung to his left and swiped at a moving shadow.

The hootch's furnishings scattered. Cots were upended, and thrown about. A helmet hit Sau Ban's chest, fell harmlessly at his feet. Everyone seemed to be screaming.

"What the fuck!" Monroe yelled in disbelief. He'd taken the grazing blow on the shoulder, a chunk of meat had been sliced off the top of his arm. He could feel it dangling there.

Tucker had finally located a weapon, but was afraid to shoot in the darkness. He heard the air being sliced beside his face and dove over a cot and into the aisle. He could see Sau Ban against the backdrop of screen, his hands held high, coming forward.

Tucker fired once.

The shock to Sau Ban's arm spun him around, and his only thought was escape. He ran through the door, and forgetting about the steps, toppled head-first onto the path. He staggered to his feet, then dashed in the direction of the CQ. What was left of his arm swung at his side. It was too soon for pain yet. The knife, its handle blood-wet and sticky, was still in his hand. Thoughts kept flying away from him. He'd come here to die. Why had he run when he had come to die like a warrior? Had he expected the soldiers wouldn't shoot him? But the closeness of the soldier's rifle, the way its muzzle seemed to touch his face with orange flame, these things turned him around, made him forget he was a warrior prepared to die, and his first instinct had been to flee like a coward. He told himself he should have stayed there and made them kill him. Instead he was alive and wounded. Thoughts came in a rush. It was that monkey's fault. Douh would be dead if not for that monkey. Wait! The soldiers wouldn't kill him. They would take him prisoner. Put him on a chain and parade him through the camp like a monkey. He'd be their monkey! He could feel the panic building, but couldn't seem to will it away. He knew he must be losing a lot of blood. A weakness entered his legs. He tried shaking them to life before shuffling farther behind the CQ.

If he could make it through the open stretch to the rear of the hootches, he might be able to skirt his way back to the path. The soldiers would not be looking toward the wire. If they spotted him, he still had the knife and would run at them until they stopped him for good. He summoned his strength, then dashed through the shadows for the hootches.

He'd only just gotten there and ducked underneath the place when he heard the scuffle of feet running down the path in the direction he'd just come. In a moment he was on his legs. He stumbled a bit. It was all or nothing now. Sau Ban made for the path and ran.

The sound of Tucker's shot had alerted the bunker guards along Charlie's side of the camp that something was amiss. There came the whoosh of a hand-held flare launching skyward where it burst with the sound of bottle-rocket. A small parachute of light floated back to earth. The camp's shadows ran hard beneath it.

"There," Leon whispered, pointing up the path.

The sudden brightness of the flare had startled Sau Ban. Without thinking he'd looked up to see what it was and stumbled. He was back on his feet and running again by the time Leon spotted him.

"It's him, ain't it, Doe-doe," Tucker whispered.

"Who else could it be?" Douh whispered back.

"Fucker is crazy," Tucker said.

"Maybe we oughta sound the alarm?" Leon asked.

"And have everybody shooting each other in the dark?" Tucker flicked on the flashlight and beamed light at their feet. The rice knife lay there, its handle and blade smeared red. Several drops of blood led away from it.

"Leon, go back and see about Monroe. Get him to the aid-station. Me and Douh are gonna follow this blood trail. That bastard ain't going very far like this."

He ran in a stagger now, no longer caring if he was seen. He couldn't think beyond the pain, the flow of it, the way it faded, only to come back with mind-numbing intensity. Sau Ban bit his tongue to stifle the scream burning in his throat. He could taste blood. His vision blurred. Shadows folded together as one. He concentrated on putting one foot in front of the other. With each step Sau Ban believed he was moving farther away from his destination. He couldn't feel his legs. For a time he thought he could see a small animal hopping in front of him. He chased after it until it vanished. The night air felt cold on his face, chilled him even as he ran. The path seemed to be rising suddenly upward. He focused on the stars wrapped in blue space, watched them draw closer. He tripped over the first pile of ammo boxes when he came to them. His legs would no longer support him, so he crawled. He hadn't bothered to cover the hole—he wasn't coming back—and found it easily.

It took a while to fumble the flashlight to life. Sau Ban gripped the L-shaped light with his good hand and started the long crawl to Tay Ninh's. He became mesmerized by the light playing over the narrow tube ahead. He imagined the tunnel an orange throat, an artery. Everything seemed off level. He stopped recognizing floor from wall and lost the sense of up and down. Sau Ban told himself to follow the light. It's going where I want to go, I'll let it take me there, he thought. Things were fading in and out of clear. Delirious thoughts bounced behind his eyes.

The blood-trail was easy enough to follow. Every few paces they came across another drop or two. Tucker and Douh eased along behind it, one eye out for Sau Ban. Only the bunker guards seemed concerned that a weapon had been fired in the camp. A single shot inside a hootch late at night could mean a lot of things, Tucker knew, and most of them bad. Taking a look to see how bad was always a job for someone else. But Tucker couldn't believe he and Douh hadn't come across Sau Ban's body yet. How a person could keep going after losing as much blood as he'd been looking at was beyond him. But then the trail went cold. Tucker paced a wide circle. Nothing. He beamed the light up the path to where it ended at the artillery dump. His palms were sweating. The rifle's grip went slick in his hand.

Some of the ammo boxes had been stacked in the dump, others lay about the area in heaps. Tucker had never visited the place before and was surprised at their numbers.

"Stay out on the edge in case he tries to run out, Doe-doe," Tucker whispered before ducking behind a stack and inching his way in.

At first he only stood and listened. After a while he flashed the light here and there. When Tucker caught a smear of blood on one of the boxes, he moved to it. There was more blood on the other side, like something had been drug there. Tucker shined the beam along the blood to where it ended on the sunken hole in the ground, and couldn't believe what he was seeing.

"Good god," he whispered, then yelled for Douh.

There were voices now. The flashlight was gone, and there was nothing ahead but light. Reach it, the voices said. Glowing, beckoning light, more lovely than any he had ever seen. It spilled into the tunnel like golden water rushing to meet him. The voices spoke of other things. Leaves drifting along a gutter. Leaves floating above the dust. This is where they went, the voices said, and he was being taken forward to be with them. He rolled to his back, swam in the light, turned his face to its brilliance, let it carry him. But up there. Up there was the source of the light. The light the voices said would heal him. With the last of his strength Sau Ban struggled to his knees. His fingers clawed dirt. He was standing. The light touched his skin. Warmed it like fire until he saw her and the fire went cold. She was there. Watching. The resurrected Tay Ninh. The living Tay Ninh, moving spirit-like in front of the light until it was hidden from him. There were no sounds left to hear. Only an approaching silence. The air went flat in his chest. He held out his arm at the moment Tay Ninh's hand squeezed the detonator. The claymore at his feet exploded, and a thousand steel balls carried pieces of Sau Ban into the night.

The old tunnel collapsed a little at a time, folding in on itself like a finger stroking a line in the dirt. The explosion in Tay Ninh's house brought everyone from their sleep, and soon the area around the artillery dump was swarming with soldiers, all trying to look at the tunnel, all waving flashlights to see what their friends said they'd seen. Dawn was approaching.

A short time earlier the medics had come for Boyle. Tucker met them on his way back to the company area, a bulky body bag hanging between them. One of the medics kept clearing his throat and spitting sickly to the side.

More than anything Tucker wanted a smoke. He eased himself down on the hootch steps, lit a cigarette, dangled it between his knees. He was as tired as he'd ever been in his life. It was work just to bring the cigarette to his lips.

Monroe was gone, too. Tucker hadn't gotten the chance to say good-bye. Leon told him the medics said the blade had gone all the way to bone, chipping it like a whittler's mark. It looked like the kind of wound that meant Monroe was going home.

Tucker hoped so. He had the feeling he would most likely never see Monroe again. But that was okay. He would just as soon remember him the way he was, here, when everything meant more than it ever would back home.

Leon and Douh were inside the hootch sitting on Leon's cot. Bastard was on the floor a short distance away, once more nibbling the edges of a cookie. Conroy's radio was turned to a low volume on his footlocker. The weatherman said there would be rain in the delta for several more days. The new year was coming.

Tucker got to his feet and stood in the doorway, both hands shoved in his pockets. The tattoo smelled rancid and ill. The aidstation. He'd go there in a little while and have it taken care of.

The sun broke free of the horizon. Around the camp, mist rose in ghostly white clouds from the paddies, while treelines ran their shadows out to join them. Sunlight played over the front of the latrine, and Tucker watched as a wedge of orange inched along one of its screens. The fly was there. Big and black as ever. Warming himself. His wings buzzing at first light.

ELEGY

Into sunlight they marched,
into dog day, into no saints day,
and were cut down.
They marched without knowing
how the air would be sucked from their lungs,
how their lungs would collapse,
how the world would twist itself, would
bend into the cruel angles.
Into the black understanding they marched
until the angels came
calling their names,
until they rose, one by one from the blood.
The light blasted down on them.
The bullets sliced through the razor grass
so there was not even time to speak.
The words would not let themselves be spoken.
Some of them died.
Some of them were not allowed to.

Bruce Weigl

Robert David Clark was born and raised in a small town in central Iowa, where, in May 1968, Uncle Sam found him and requested his presence for the next two years. He served in Vietnam from 1968-1969 as a light weapons infantryman. After his discharge from the army he attended Minnesota State University, at Mankato, where he lives with his two daughters. While attending MSU, he won the Robert Wright writing scholarship, and an Associated Writing Programs award for fiction. *Flowers of the Dinh Ba Forest* is his first published novel.